The

Lord Chamberlain's

Daughter

A Novel By

Ron Fritsch

ISBN: 978-0997882971

Published by Asymmetric Worlds

For information, address:

Asymmetric Worlds
1657 West Winona Street
Chicago, IL 60640-2707

Front cover photo by Kharchenko-irina7

For David, Lee Ann and my family

The Characters

Christina, the Swedish ambassador to Denmark

Claudius, a prince of Denmark, the elder Hamlet's brother, the younger Hamlet's uncle, Gertrude's brother-in-law

Eric, Claudius's servant

Fortinbras, the prince of Norway

Gertrude, the queen of Denmark, the younger Hamlet's mother, the elder Hamlet's wife, Claudius's sister-in-law

Hamlet the elder, the king of Denmark, Prince Hamlet's father, Claudius's brother, Gertrude's husband

Hamlet the younger, a prince of Denmark, King Hamlet's son, Claudius's nephew, Gertrude's son

Horatio, a friend of Prince Hamlet, Ophelia and Laertes who works in the royal stable

Laertes, Ophelia's brother, Polonius's son

Ophelia, Polonius's daughter, Laertes's sister

Polonius, the lord chamberlain of Denmark, Ophelia and Laertes's father

Chapter One

The Visit

As soon as Fortinbras learned Ophelia was still alive, he sent her a message asking if he could pay her a visit. He surprised her when he arrived at her cottage. He wore a shirt and trousers a farmer would wear. He was on a horse he'd ridden from Elsinore Castle alone.

He dismounted without taking his eyes off her. "I was told you'd thrown yourself into a river and drowned. People said you must've washed out to sea. That's why nobody found your body."

Ophelia gave her guest a wan smile. "That was the story people told about me. I'm glad, of course, it wasn't true."

"There was talk you were despondent because your brother and father and Prince Hamlet had been killed."

"That was the story people told."

The summer day Fortinbras had chosen for his visit was warm and sunny. Ophelia invited him to sit with her on a bench in the shade of an apple tree at the edge of her orchard. They had a view of a pasture enclosed by a wooden fence. Fortinbras's horse, tethered to the tree, munched on the orchard grass behind them.

When Ophelia was a child, other youngsters at the castle often told her she and her brother Laertes didn't look like Danes. With their dark brown hair, almond eyes and slender physiques, they could've passed for children of the servants who attended the ambassadors from Greece, Italy and Spain.

Ophelia doubted anybody ever questioned whether Fortinbras was a true Scandinavian. He was blond, blue-eyed and tall. He was as fit, at thirty-six, as the soldier he used to be—a soldier who trained, by all accounts, every day between battles.

"I often wonder," he said, "about that awful business involving your family and the royal family. I've heard the story that goes around. But it raises so many questions. To be honest with you, I find it difficult to believe six people—two kings, a queen, a prince and two lord chamberlains—got killed the way the story says they did."

Ophelia had imagined Fortinbras would have any number of

questions for her regarding that awful business.

"For one thing," he said, "I've never been able to figure out Prince Hamlet's uncle."

Ophelia looked at the hayfield beyond the pasture and frowned. "What can't you figure out about him?"

"Everybody tells me Claudius poisoned his older brother, the king, Hamlet's father."

"That's the story people tell."

"But why did Claudius suppose he could get away with a crime so obvious? Why didn't he stop to think Prince Hamlet would surely seek revenge for the murder of his father?"

Ophelia remained silent.

"Is it possible," Fortinbras asked, "somebody else killed the king?"

Remembering all too well the death of Hamlet's father and the horrific events that followed it ten years ago, Ophelia shuddered as if she were in a dream from which waking could provide no escape.

Ophelia's Story: Seventeen Years before the Visit

In his childhood, Prince Hamlet had three close friends. Quiet, studious, well-behaved Horatio was an orphan whose parents had been servants at Elsinore Castle. The far more exuberant Laertes and Ophelia were the only children of Polonius, the lord chamberlain. Their mother had died when Ophelia was five years old and Laertes six.

The prince and his three friends roamed the castle and its grounds without any apparent restriction. They were familiar with the servants to an unusual degree. They called them by their names and knew what they did and how they did it.

Polonius couldn't conceal how pleased he was that his son and daughter were special friends of the prince, who was the only royal child in the kingdom. At the same time, though, the lord chamberlain made no attempt to hide his irritation that Horatio had somehow become, like a weed in an otherwise flawless garden, a member of their group.

One afternoon Polonius overheard Laertes complain he was too hungry to concentrate on the history lesson the royal tutor was attempting to teach the prince and his friends. Hamlet and Laertes were twelve years old. Ophelia and Horatio were eleven.

Polonius interrupted the class and told Horatio to go to the royal kitchen and bring back some food. "Like an obedient and useful servant," he chose to add.

The lord chamberlain's demand and remark incensed his daughter. "Horatio isn't our servant," she said. "When we need something to eat, we'll go get it ourselves. We know where the kitchen is. We know the cooks."

Laertes laughed. "They give us whatever we ask for."

"Ophelia's right," Hamlet said. "Horatio isn't our servant. He's our friend."

What could Polonius say after that? Hamlet was, after all, the prince.

The Visit

"Who are the people in the hayfield?" Fortinbras asked.

Ophelia smiled. "My husband and our children. They're bringing in the second crop of the season. We cut it two days ago. Our timing was good. It dried out beautifully yesterday."

Ophelia's husband and children were forking the hay onto a low wagon a horse pulled.

"Would you be helping them," Fortinbras asked, "if I hadn't come to see you?"

Ophelia nodded. "You needn't worry about that, though. They gave me the afternoon off. They agreed I had something more important to do."

"How old are your children?"

"The older girl is nine. The boys are seven and six. The younger girl will be three by the end of the year. The others take turns watching her."

Ophelia's Story: Sixteen Years before the Visit

When Hamlet and Laertes were thirteen, and Ophelia and Horatio twelve, talk of a possible wedding a few years in the future began.

Polonius repeated the gossip with the glee of a child opening birthday presents.

"The prince and my daughter," he often said, "I can't imagine a more perfect marriage."

Laertes, on the other hand, insisted the thought of his friend and sister in bed together doing what a husband and wife did made him sick to his stomach.

Another Elsinore Castle assumption of many years standing by then was that Laertes would succeed his father as lord chamberlain.

"If you marry Hamlet," Horatio told Ophelia one day while they were riding on a clifftop above the sea, "you'll outrank your older brother."

Ophelia was on her horse. Horatio rode, as he often did, Hamlet's.

Other children never questioned whether Hamlet and Horatio were true Danes. They both had the height, stature and blond hair to prove it. Horatio's eyes were as dark as Ophelia's, and often as brooding, but nobody held that against him.

"Your brother," he said, "will have to bow down to you the same as the rest of us will. He admitted to me he'll never feel right doing that."

Ophelia laughed. "That's the silliest thing I've ever heard. If I married Hamlet, Laertes and I would still be brother and sister."

"But would you favor him?"

"Just because he was my brother? Absolutely not."

"See?"

Ophelia rode off on her white horse at a gallop.

Horatio continued trotting his. He and Ophelia both knew he wasn't the rider she was. Somewhere along the way, they also knew, she'd stop, view the waves crashing against the rocks below the cliff, and wait for him to catch up with her. She especially liked one spot where she could watch wave after wave enter a cavern in the rocks and come spilling out again.

The Visit

Fortinbras gestured toward the cattle, sheep and goats grazing in the pasture. "I was told you'd become a farmer."

Ophelia nodded. "My aunt, my mother's sister, left me this farm. She never married or had any children of her own. After my mother died, my aunt moved to Elsinore to raise Laertes and me. She and my father, though, despised one another. Soon after the war began, she came back here to live."

Fortinbras closed his eyes and shook his head. "That war."

"That stupid, horrible war."

Hamlet's father, himself called Hamlet, had begun the war when Ophelia was nine years old. He did it after the king of Norway,

Fortinbras's father, had rejected the Danish demand that he give up certain territories his royal ancestors had supposedly stolen from Denmark.

Fortinbras sighed. "If the kings of Denmark ever ruled those territories, it must've been an awfully long time ago. The people living in them have spoken Norwegian for many generations now."

Ophelia nodded. "The king and my father had a plan to deal with that. They were going to throw your Norwegians out and replace them with Danes. That's how they got the lords to agree to fight the war. The king promised he'd divide the new territories among them after your Norwegians were gone."

"Our people living in those parts assumed that would happen. That's why they put up such fierce resistance. They told one another they had to help our army fight off the Danish invaders. Otherwise, they'd end up in the sea."

"We heard about that. The Norwegians our army tried to uproot did every sneaky thing they could to stop us. They hijacked our supply wagons in the forests. They shot flaming arrows into our encampments and set them on fire. But the king and my father refused to listen when our commanding officers complained. My father told them the common people, especially the Norwegians, could never be a threat to a well-trained, well-led army."

Fortinbras laughed. "Especially the Norwegians?"

Ophelia's Story: Fifteen Years before the Visit

The fourteen-year-old prince and Laertes and thirteen-year-old Ophelia and Horatio were at the farm the summer day five mounted knights showed up.

Ophelia's aunt had taught Ophelia and Horatio how to milk her cows, ewes and nannies and make the cheese she sold.

The war had gone on then for more than four years, like an illness beyond hope of either recovery or death.

The captain of the knights, still on his horse, spoke with Ophelia's aunt not far from the bench beneath a young apple tree. "We've got orders for two of your steers."

Ophelia's aunt nodded. "I've got two steers I planned to take to market next week. Will you pay me what I'd get for them there?"

The captain shook his head. "We've got no money to pay you for your steers."

As if she were mimicking the captain, Ophelia's aunt shook her head. "You'll have to leave then without the steers."

"We've got orders," the captain said, "to take two of your steers. They'll go to Norway. We need them to feed our comrades who're fighting and dying there."

Ophelia's aunt shook her head again. "You'll need to pay me for them."

"We're taking steers from all the farmers in this area," the captain said. "You and your neighbors can consider them your contribution to the war effort."

Ophelia stepped forward. "What if my aunt doesn't want to make a contribution to the war effort? What if she thinks we should let the Norwegians be and bring your comrades home to Denmark safe and sound?"

"Then your aunt's a traitor," the captain replied, "and deserves to have her head chopped off."

Ophelia gasped.

The captain turned to Ophelia's aunt. "Now show us those two steers you were thinking of taking to the market. Those are the ones we need for our comrades in Norway."

The knights rode to the nearest gate to the pasture, which wasn't far from the apple tree. Two of them dismounted and opened the gate.

Ophelia motioned to Hamlet, Laertes and Horatio to follow her. She and they ran around the knights, through the gateway and into the pasture.

In an attempt to keep the knights from confiscating the steers, they placed themselves between the swordsmen and the cattle herd.

"You aren't taking steers from this farm," Ophelia declared.

"I'm the prince," Hamlet informed the knights.

"I'm the lord chamberlain's son," Laertes said.

"And I'm the lord chamberlain's daughter," Ophelia said. "Our fathers would never permit this to happen."

The captain and the other knights drew and brandished their swords.

"Your fathers," the captain said, "told us themselves we're to take the steers."

"And anybody who gets in our way," one of the other knights said, aiming his sword at Ophelia, "we're free to kill as a traitor."

Ophelia spat at the sword. "You aren't going to kill the prince as a traitor. You aren't going to kill the lord chamberlain's son and daughter as traitors."

The captain aimed his sword at Horatio. "Who are you?"

"He's Horatio," Ophelia said. "He's our friend."

"Ophelia," her aunt called to her, "step aside. All of you, step aside. Let the knights take the steers. They have swords. We don't."

Ophelia stepped aside. She realized, as her aunt had, the knights could kill Horatio and teach the prince and the lord chamberlain's son and daughter a damned good lesson about what their fathers' swordsmen could and would do.

Chapter Two

Ophelia's Story: Fifteen Years before the Visit

By the time the prince and his friends returned to Elsinore Castle that evening, Ophelia had persuaded Hamlet to take them to see his father in his chamber.

The king greeted them, as they knew he would, sitting stiffly in his highbacked wooden chair as if he were holding court in the throne room. Queen Gertrude and Uncle Claudius sat on either side of him in the far more comfortable cushioned chairs they preferred.

The prince and his friends also knew his father expected them to bow and curtsy when they saw him and address him as Your Majesty or Your Highness.

After they did so, Ophelia described what they'd observed earlier that day at her aunt's farm. "I never thought," she said, "I'd see our knights stealing livestock from our farmers."

As was so often the case, Polonius, hovering near the king like a shadow, did most of the talking for him. "We can't let our army go hungry," he said, glaring at his daughter as if she were a servant who'd spoken out of turn.

The lord chamberlain's white hair, which hung to his shoulders, used to be as dark brown as his children's.

Ophelia gave her father a dismissive look. "My aunt told me the king and the lords are supposed to buy steers at the markets to feed their knights in Norway. They're not allowed to steal what they need from the farmers."

The lord chamberlain peered at his daughter through narrowed eyes. "His Majesty has decided the common people need to pay their fair share of the expenses of our fighting to make Denmark whole again. Otherwise, we'll lose the war. Then those bloodthirsty Norwegians will come here and kill us all. Is that what you want?"

Ophelia scoffed. "Of course not. If we lost the war, why wouldn't we just bring our army home and be done with it? Why would the Norwegians need to come here and kill us?"

Her father's eyes were contracted to slits. "To get back at us for starting the war."

"For revenge," the king said. "They'd do it for revenge."

He was dressed from his cravat to his shoes, as he always was, in black. So was Polonius. Their children often referred to them as the raven king and the raven lord chamberlain.

Gertrude and Claudius, though, wore garments whose bright colors played off the other's like flowers in a whimsical garden.

Polonius wasn't done with his daughter. "The knights' captain told you what I would've told you. Anybody who opposes feeding our army is an enemy to the kingdom, a traitor who deserves to die. And we can't and don't make exceptions for children who foolishly think they know better than their parents."

The king turned to his son and shrugged.

Ophelia had seen him do it in court. Her father the lord chamberlain would find wanting some unfortunate supplicant's plea, and there was nothing His Majesty could do about it.

"Now leave us," Polonius said. "The king has far more important matters to spend his time on than a couple of damned steers."

But his daughter also wasn't done. "Taking livestock from farmers without paying for them is wrong. It's theft, no matter who does it."

"I told you to leave us!" her father barked. "Go now, or I'll call for the guards to remove you! And I'll order them to give you all a good cuffing on your way out!"

Gertrude and Claudius glanced at one another and laughed.

"Farewell, little children," the queen chose to say.

Two of the little children, Hamlet and Horatio, were taller than she was.

The Visit

"That was just the beginning of the confiscations," Ophelia said. "The knights came back for more and more steers. And after they took all the steers, they came for the heifers and the sheep and the goats."

"We heard that in Norway," Fortinbras said.

Ophelia's Story: Fourteen Years before the Visit

After five years of fighting, the Danish forces had recovered less than a third of the territories their king and lord chamberlain had claimed belonged to Denmark. But the war was costing the Danes far more in treasure, casualties and deaths than the king and his highest official had imagined it would.

Hiding behind curtains in her father's chamber, Ophelia overheard them conceding that point on more than one occasion. Then she heard them say they no longer had enough knights under their command to continue the fighting. That admission, though, didn't lead them to stop the war.

Ophelia's Story: Thirteen Years before the Visit

Fifteen-year-old Horatio reported to his friends what had happened to a servant who'd worked with him in the royal stable. Knights with drawn swords had come to his family's cottage in the middle of the night. They informed the youth, who'd recently celebrated his seventeenth birthday, he could either volunteer to fight for his country in Norway or face an immediate execution for treason. They said they'd bury him far out at sea in a net with boulders weighing it down to ensure they'd never have to explain the existence of his corpse.

His family argued with the knights at length and with great passion, but they achieved nothing. The knights had orders from their commanding officer to take the youth, dead or alive.

His parents and siblings ultimately had to talk him into volunteering for the war. They'd heard it was going badly, but that choice at least gave him a chance to survive.

Abducting knights, as the people soon called them, came looking for other sons of servants and farmers between the ages of seventeen and twenty-five and forced them to go with them to Norway. The young men who chose to hide from their captors soon learned that countermeasure wouldn't wake them from their nightmare. The knights took a younger brother, sister or cousin they threatened to kill if the youth they wanted didn't give himself up.

Ophelia's Story: Thirteen Years before the Visit

Hamlet and his friends went to his father again, this time to demand he put an end to the abduction of fighting-age servants and farmers.

"Nobody can believe, Your Majesty," Ophelia said to the raven king, "you'd allow the knights to force young men to fight in a war. The people think you should order them to bring those men home to their families."

The king, though, chose to state his position using as few words as he could. "We're fighting a war."

"You're damned right," Claudius said.

Hamlet's uncle didn't surprise Ophelia with his remark. He wanted no one to doubt his fervor for regaining the stolen territories was as intense as his brother's. He knew he had no price to pay for his bluster. He wasn't the king. The war wasn't his to lose.

Polonius sneered at his daughter and her friends. "And children all choked up with tears in their eyes don't make decisions for kings fighting wars. Those men taken to Norway should've volunteered to fight for their king and country in the first place. Loyal subjects don't need to be forced to do their duty."

Gertrude nodded. "The king needs to do everything he can to win the war."

Polonius had long ago told Ophelia the queen had strongly favored the war when it was still only an idea in the king's mind. By recapturing the territories previous kings had lost to the war-loving Norwegians and making Denmark whole again, Hamlet's father would become the greatest Danish king in history. All the other figures appearing in the annals of Denmark would seem insignificant next to him. And Gertrude would be remembered and cherished as the queen who'd inspired King Hamlet the Great to achieve his colossal victory.

The Visit

Ophelia turned from her family working in the hayfield to her guest sitting with her on a bench under an apple tree. "Did you ever order your knights to abduct young men to fight in the war?"

Fortinbras, staring at a honeybee that had used the back of his hand for a resting place between the clover in the pasture and its hive, scowled. "No, we never did that."

Ophelia knew her guest's story. He was seventeen years old, only eight years older than she was, when Denmark invaded Norway. On the day the enemy army landed on its beaches, his father appointed him to take command of the Norwegian army.

The raven king and lord chamberlain had never imagined the Norwegian king's response to their invasion would be so foolhardy. They didn't know the prince, motherless from his birth, had spent the last five years of his life, at his request, training with the army. During that time, he shared quarters and took all his meals with its highest commanders. When they learned the Danish ships were sailing for Norway, they asked the king to place Fortinbras in charge.

"Why'd you choose to enter the army at such an early age?" Ophelia asked.

Fortinbras couldn't take his eyes off the bee. "That was when your king began threatening our ambassador to Denmark. Your king and your father said my father could either hand over the stolen territories or Denmark would take them back by force of arms. I knew neither my father nor any other king of Norway could ever agree to give up any territory many generations of Norwegians had called their home. So I wanted to be ready when your king made good on his threat."

The army Prince Fortinbras led suffered far fewer casualties and deaths during the first years of the war than the invaders did. His knights fought defensively on territories well-known to them but unfamiliar to their opponents. He wasn't reluctant to give up a parcel of land in order to save the lives of his warriors. But he did so only after he'd made the Danes pay the highest possible price for it.

Early in the sixth year of the war, Denmark's incremental progress into Norway came to an end. The raven king and lord chamberlain in Elsinore Castle refused to accept the first reports of the halt. They went so far as to remind the messengers from the front line they could be charged with treason for spreading false rumors regarding the war. Ophelia heard her father say he'd more readily believe the couriers if they tried to tell him the sun had stopped in its passage across the sky.

Then, even more unbelievably, young Fortinbras began recovering the regions he'd given up. He proved to be as methodical on offense as he'd been on defense.

Ophelia watched the well-rested bee arise from the back of her guest's hand and resume its flight to its hive. "The story our people told was that you only fought battles you knew you'd win. They said you were like a fox choosing its prey."

Fortinbras laughed. "I only fought battles my commanders and I thought our fighters had a damned good chance to win."

"Our people said you took your time at it, too."

"If we'd tried to hurry things, we would've lost too many well-trained and loyal fighters. Your father and your king proved to us the folly of relying upon abducted boys to do the fighting."

"Is it true, whenever you captured those boys, you let them go free?"

"We told them they could stay in Norway. With the war on and so many of our people helping at the front, we had a lot of work for our Danish guests to do, as long as it was their choice to do it. I understand most of them are still in Norway."

"Speaking Norwegian?"

Fortinbras looked at Ophelia and smiled. "I've heard that's what they speak now."

He was King Hamlet's nephew and Prince Hamlet's first cousin. King Hamlet had two siblings. One was his younger brother Claudius. The other was an older sister. Their father had arranged her marriage to the youth who was then the prince of Norway and later became the king. She died giving birth to their first and only child, Fortinbras. He was therefore not only first in the line of succession to the Norwegian throne. He was also third in the line of succession to the Danish throne. Only Prince Hamlet and Prince Claudius ranked higher than him.

Ophelia's Story: Twelve Years before the Visit

It became a rule in Denmark that when boys turned seventeen, they could either show up at Elsinore Castle and volunteer for duty, or they could wait at home for angry knights to come for them. But they all went to Norway, many to die within a few months of their arrival.

As Hamlet and Laertes approached their seventeenth birthdays, they increasingly worried they'd have to volunteer themselves.

Laertes beat his fist on Hamlet's card table. "This fucked-up war can't possibly be over before we turn seventeen."

He, the prince, Ophelia and Horatio were in Hamlet's chamber playing cards.

"We'll come home dead," Hamlet agreed. "Or maybe they'll just bury us in Norway."

Laertes grimaced. "Or let us rot where we fall."

"We'd better go see our fathers," Ophelia said. "Maybe they'll come to their senses and stop the damned war—rather than risk the lives of their own sons."

Entering the king's chamber, the prince and his friends bowed and curtsied once again. King Hamlet, Queen Gertrude, Prince Claudius and Lord Chamberlain Polonius were in their usual places.

After hearing the pleas of his son and Laertes, the king wasted few words on his response. "We won't stop the war. Not until we've accomplished everything we set out to do."

Uncle Claudius was no less brief. "No matter what it takes."

Polonius nodded. "And we've already spent too much on the war to stop it now. We've lost too many men in it to even consider stopping it now."

"I don't understand what you're saying," Ophelia said. "If you've spent too much treasure on your war and lost too many men in it to stop it now, when will you ever be able to stop it?"

Polonius looked at his daughter as if she'd produced a sword and was prepared to run him through with it. "We'll stop the war," he replied, "when we've won it."

Ophelia shook her head. "You aren't winning it now."

The prince and Laertes looked at her as if she'd appeared out of nowhere.

"And I'm certain as hell," she continued, "you'll never win it."

Horatio seemed to be the only person in the king's chamber Ophelia hadn't startled.

And she wasn't done. "So you'll even throw away your sons in your hopeless damned war? And here I thought parents were supposed to love their sons."

"Stop!" her father yelled at her. "Stop your treasonous talk! Leave us! Get out of here! All of you! I'll call the guards to take you out! And give you the damned good thrashings you need! Each of you!"

Ophelia's Story: Twelve Years before the Visit

Later that evening, the king sent a messenger asking the prince and Laertes to return to his chamber.

"Can Ophelia and Horatio come with us?" Hamlet asked.

The messenger shrugged. "Your father didn't say."

"We'll all go," Hamlet said.

The king spoke as soon as Hamlet and Laertes entered his chamber.

"We've decided what to do with you. Neither of you will be in Denmark when you turn seventeen. The knights won't come looking for you."

"Where will we be?" Hamlet asked.

"You'll be in Wittenberg," the king replied, "pursuing your studies."

Ophelia and Horatio took turns throwing their arms around Hamlet and Laertes.

"We'll miss you both," Ophelia said, "but you'll be safe."

"That's what counts," Horatio added.

"You'll be safe in Germany," Polonius said, "but only on one condition."

"And what condition is that?" Ophelia asked.

"That none of you," Polonius replied, "say another word against the war. Not one word. Either to the king, the queen, Prince Claudius or me. And certainly not to the public."

Ophelia took a deep breath. "I'll agree not to say another word against that horrible war. But only to keep the prince and my brother safe from it."

Chapter Three

The Visit

"That's what the king and my father were afraid of the most," Ophelia said. "The people had heard the prince and the lord chamberlain's daughter and son opposed the war as much as the families of military-age men did."

"But the four of you accepted your father's condition?" Fortinbras asked.

Ophelia nodded. "Each of us promised we'd never say another word against the war. Horatio and I knew we were lying."

"But Hamlet and Laertes?"

"I'm not certain what they were thinking then. I do know they were awfully glad they weren't going to fight in the war themselves."

Ophelia's Story: Twelve Years before the Visit

Ophelia, though, wasn't satisfied with the exemptions from the war for Hamlet and Laertes. "What about Horatio?" she asked. "What happens to him when he turns seventeen?"

Polonius glared at his daughter. "We don't send the sons of servants to study in foreign lands. Stable boys can always hope the war ends in a great victory for Denmark before they turn seventeen. Otherwise, they can damned well do their duty and volunteer to fight the Norwegians."

Ophelia took Horatio in her arms. "Never," she whispered in his ear. "I'll never let that happen."

Out of the corner of her eye, Ophelia could see Gertrude shifting in her chair as if to relieve a sudden discomfort in the area of her buttocks.

The queen turned to Polonius. "Would you mind, lord chamberlain, if I addressed your daughter regarding her conduct?"

"Not at all," Polonius replied. "She's obviously a daughter whose conduct needs addressing."

"But I don't believe," Gertrude said, "the young men will need to hear what I say."

"The young men," Polonius said, "will therefore leave us."

Hamlet, Laertes and Horatio, all seeming perplexed, left the king's chamber.

The queen turned to Ophelia. “Your youth no longer gives you an excuse.”

“An excuse?” Ophelia asked. “An excuse for what?”

“For spending far too much of your time,” Gertrude replied, “in the company of a male servant who works in the royal stable—a rough boy you even dare to bring with you when you call upon the king in his chamber.”

“I couldn’t agree more, Your Majesty,” Polonius said. “And when my daughter does that, she brings nothing but shame down on her family.”

Ophelia couldn’t imagine bringing more shame down on her family than her father had. He’d ordered the seizure without payment of the farmers’ livestock and the forced military service of young men who’d never trained to fight a war.

“The prince asks Horatio to come with us,” Ophelia said. “So does Laertes. They both consider him their best friend. What am I supposed to do? Tell the prince and my brother they can’t bring their best friend with them? They’d laugh at me.”

Gertrude scoffed. “I see what I see. Horatio appears to be as friendly to you as he is to the prince and your brother.”

“I suppose he is,” Ophelia said. “So what?”

Polonius turned to Ophelia. “My child, you’re speaking to the queen. I suggest you do so with a respectful tone in your voice.”

Ophelia chose to ignore her father.

“I might also add,” the king said, “I can no longer permit my son’s future bride to be seen in public with a male servant. Not unless he’s strictly performing a servant’s duties.”

“Who says,” Ophelia asked the king, “I’m your son’s future bride?”

“I say it,” the king replied.

“As do I,” Polonius said.

“In this time of war,” the king said, “I feel it’s absolutely necessary for the royal family and the lord chamberlain’s family to show the people their solidarity. Nothing we do can speak louder on that subject than your marriage to the prince.”

“That’s all fine and well,” Ophelia said, “but I haven’t yet chosen to be Prince Hamlet’s bride. I could choose to marry him, but then again I could choose not to.”

The queen knitted her brow. "What makes you think you have a choice in the matter?"

"She needs to learn," Polonius said, "she doesn't have a choice—not when it comes to her marriage."

Gertrude gave the king a glance that appeared to Ophelia as clouded with regret as a picnic outing on a rainy summer day.

"None of the three adults in this room who married," the queen said, "chose the person they married. In your case, I think my son is more than fit to be your husband."

"I don't question his fitness," Ophelia said.

"Then we have no more need," the king said, "to speak of this matter. I'll announce tomorrow in court your betrothal to Hamlet. When he returns to Denmark from his studies in Wittenberg, he and you will become husband and wife."

The Visit

"Did your father ever attempt to choose a wife for you?" Ophelia asked her guest.

Fortinbras shook his head. "He knew he'd never get away with it. I married my wife because I loved her."

"Did she choose you?"

"I never would've married her if I hadn't thought she wanted me as much as I wanted her."

Ophelia could see her husband and children had fully loaded the wagon with hay.

Fortinbras looked at Ophelia and smiled. "My wife was as glad as I was to learn you were still alive. She asked me to extend her greetings to you. She'd like to see you again."

"I'd like to see her again, too. I'd also like to meet your children. I understand you have three about the same ages as mine."

Fortinbras nodded. "We'll have a get-together for them."

Ophelia's Story: Twelve Years before the Visit

After the king's announcement in the throne room regarding Prince Hamlet's future marriage to the lord chamberlain's daughter, Hamlet chose to walk with Ophelia to her chamber.

She made no attempt to seem a happy bride-to-be.

"Aren't you pleased?" Hamlet asked.

"About what? That you and Laertes won't have to fight in Norway? Yes, I'm very pleased our fathers have decided to send you to Wittenberg instead."

"I was thinking, though, about something else."

"What might that be?"

Hamlet looked at Ophelia as if she'd slapped him. "Our marriage," he replied. "It's no longer childish speculation. Our fathers have agreed it will really happen."

Ophelia came to a halt outside the door to her chamber. "To be honest with you, being forced into a marriage doesn't please me at all. I can't imagine why anybody would think it did."

Hamlet shook his head. "We don't have to feel we're being forced to do anything."

"When the king and my father tell me—order me—who to marry, why wouldn't I feel I'm being forced?"

"Not if we want to get married anyway."

Ophelia took a deep breath. "You need to know something. Despite all that childish speculation we used to think was so funny, I don't want to marry you."

"You don't?"

Hamlet appeared to be close to tears.

"I like you as a friend," Ophelia replied. "But no, I don't want to marry you. I hope you and your father and mother can find some other suitable and willing bride for you. I'll gladly be a bridesmaid at your wedding. I'll hope she's a beautiful princess you fall madly in love with. You deserve nothing less. But no, I don't want to marry you."

While Hamlet remained standing in the hallway, Ophelia entered her chamber and closed the door behind her. How long he stood there with that disappointed-prince look on his face, she could only guess.

Ophelia's Story: Twelve Years before the Visit

The prospective marriage of Ophelia and Hamlet, growing from childhood talk like a sapling the size of a weed becoming a tree, infuriated Laertes. After the king's announcement, he refused to speak with either his sister or the prince.

He told his father he'd rather not go to Wittenberg for his studies. He'd prefer to spend his time in Paris and learn French. He didn't tell Polonius he wanted to separate himself from the prince. He claimed he simply didn't like Germans. His father granted his request.

Ophelia stood in front of her brother, blocking his passage in the hallway between their chambers in Elsinore Castle. "I don't want to marry Hamlet," she said.

Laertes scoffed. "You liar. Our father and the king have decided you'll marry the prince. And you'll gladly do what they tell you to do. You'll be the queen. Hamlet's so obsessed with you, you'll have this kingdom in the palm of your hand. He'll give every order and lay down every rule you want him to. And don't try to tell me you don't know that."

"I'm telling you I don't want to marry Hamlet. I have no wish whatsoever to be his wife. Nor do I have any desire to become another Queen Gertrude. I'll do whatever it takes to get around the king's order. I want you to help me do that."

"Liar! Let me pass! Get out of my way!"

Surprised by her brother's vehemence, Ophelia stepped aside.

Ophelia's Story: Twelve Years before the Visit

Ophelia hadn't imagined how much her rejection would devastate Hamlet.

"I knew he was in love with you," Horatio said.

He and Ophelia were in the royal stable, where, presumably, their speaking together didn't violate the rule the king had laid down for them. Horatio was doing the work he usually did, feeding oats and hay to the horses. Ophelia could always say she just happened to be in the stable at the same time grooming her horse.

"Hamlet was serious about wanting to marry me all along?"

"All along," Horatio replied. "Laertes tried to treat the matter as if it was a joke, but I could tell Hamlet was as serious about it as he's been about anything in his life."

Ophelia's Story: Twelve Years before the Visit

Ophelia's aunt became ill. Within a week she told Ophelia and

Horatio she couldn't get out of her bed by herself. Horatio immediately left the stable at Elsinore Castle and moved to the farm to care for her and do the work she otherwise would've done. Ophelia spent many of her days and nights at the farm as well.

The knights had begun taking cows to feed the army in Norway. But the next time they showed up at Ophelia's aunt's farm, all they found was a woman who told them she was on her deathbed. She said she'd sold all her livestock at the market—even her bull, ram and billy goat—because she could no longer tend them. She was grateful her kind neighbors brought her food and firewood to keep her alive.

The truth was, Horatio and Ophelia had hidden her remaining cattle, sheep and goats deep in a nearby forest. Their neighbors hid their animals in the same place so they could take turns guarding them during the night. They were still left with the daily tasks of hauling hay to feed the livestock, milking the cows, ewes and nannies where they'd hidden them, and bringing the milk home on the hay wagon.

Most of the farmers in Denmark were hiding their livestock then. They told the confiscating knights they were living off the fruits and vegetables from their orchards and gardens and whatever they could obtain hunting in the forest and fishing in the sea.

Ophelia overheard her father and the king grumble about the shameless liars the farmers had become. The two ravens acknowledged, though, they couldn't spare enough of the knights fighting in Norway to search for the missing livestock at home.

Horatio took an interest in the plants growing wild in the forest. He read all the books on botany Ophelia could find in the castle library. He paid particular attention to the herbs that were supposed to have a medicinal effect. He learned from the neighbors the plants and mushrooms they used and ate—and, of course, those they avoided. Ophelia's aunt said his potions eased her aches and pains enough for her to get a good night's sleep.

Ophelia's father and the royal family knew Ophelia was often absent from Elsinore Castle because she was caring for her aunt. They were unaware, though, that Horatio was living on her aunt's farm.

"They don't pay any attention to what the common people do," Ophelia told her aunt and Horatio, "as long as they keep themselves out of sight."

She and Horatio still worried that Hamlet and Laertes might be curious about the person they both considered their best friend, but they were distracted then, preparing to leave Elsinore Castle.

Ophelia's Story: Twelve Years before the Visit

Hamlet came to see Ophelia in her chamber the day before he was scheduled to depart for Wittenberg.

"I hope you enjoy your studies," she said, without inviting him to take a seat. "Do you intend to learn German?"

"I'm not here," Hamlet said, "to talk about my studies."

"What are you here to talk about?"

"I'm here to remind you what will happen when the damned war is over and I come home."

"I'm certain your father and mother will be very pleased to see you again. So will the people. I don't need to be reminded of that."

"There's something else you apparently do need to be reminded of."

"What might that be?"

"You and I will marry. We'll be husband and wife. We'll live together. We'll sleep together. We'll raise children together."

Ophelia took a deep breath. "I'm sorry, but I've told you before, I don't want to marry you."

"My father and your father have said you'll marry me. They'll order you to marry me. You can't defy them."

"I guarantee you I'll do everything I can to defy them. I'm not like your mother. I'll never gladly marry and sleep with a man I don't wish to marry and sleep with."

"Do you wish to marry and sleep with some other man?"

"No."

"You'd better be telling the truth. My father and your father have told me they'll never approve your marriage to another man. They'll only approve your marriage to me."

"Then I'll never marry."

"Never marry? I can't believe you'd go through life without marrying anyone. You'd become a spinster."

"I'd much rather become a spinster than the wife of a man I didn't love."

"You'd end up living in a home with other unmarried women."

Ophelia shrugged. “I might be happy doing that.”

She took Hamlet by his arm and led him to the door.

“Goodbye now,” she said, opening the door. “Have a safe trip to Wittenberg. I think you’ll enjoy your studies more if you learn to speak and write German.”

“Why are you doing this?” Hamlet asked, standing in the hallway again. “I always thought you wanted to marry me. I always thought you wanted to be the wife of a prince.”

“You were badly mistaken. I’ve never wanted to marry you. I’ve never wanted to be the wife of a prince.”

She closed the door.

Chapter Four

Ophelia's Story: Twelve Years before the Visit

Ophelia went to see her brother the day before he was scheduled to leave for France.

Laertes stood in the doorway blocking her entrance into his chamber.

"What do you want?" he asked.

"I came to wish you a safe trip to France," she replied.

"You came to gloat."

Ophelia rolled her eyes. "Gloat about what?"

"Becoming the queen. Ruling the land. Rubbing my nose in it."

"Hasn't Hamlet told you I don't wish to marry him?"

"He's never told me that. You'll marry him, he says. You have no other choice."

"That's what he tells you?"

"He doesn't tell me anything now. I choose not to speak with him. I only hear what he tells other people."

"You and he used to be friends."

"When we were children, I stupidly thought he was my friend. That's all gone to hell. We're grown up now. And you'll become the queen. You'll convince Hamlet you and he won't need a lord chamberlain. I'll end up in the stable, forking horseshit with Horatio."

Ophelia had to admit the image of her brother cleaning a stable, perhaps even being shat upon as he was bent over with his pitchfork hard at work, amused her.

"Have a safe trip," she said. "I hope you learn to speak and write French."

Laertes closed the door to his chamber and brought to an end his and his sister's childhoods.

The Visit

"That was when the resistance began," Ophelia said. "When the people learned the king and the queen and the lord chamberlain had sent their sons out of the country to avoid fighting in the war. That's when it began."

"We heard about your resistance in Norway," Fortinbras said. "The fighters we captured told us about it. Most of them regretted it hadn't happened soon enough to keep them out of the war."

Ophelia nodded. "The blatant hypocrisy angered the people. The war was well worth the lives of the sons of the common people, but it wasn't at all worth risking the lives of the sons of the king and lord chamberlain."

"Did you take part in the resistance?"

Ophelia laughed. Fortinbras might just as well have asked her if it was true she'd lived to the present day without ending her life early.

"The first youth we set out to save from the war lived near here," she replied. "Horatio and I went with him and his family to see their neighbors. Almost all of them agreed with us the time had come to stop the abductions. Everybody knew a youth who'd been forced to fight in Norway and got killed. I'd never seen the people so enraged."

"What did the people do?"

"They kept an eye on the roads. As soon as they spotted the knights approaching, they sent their children who ran the fastest to tell their neighbors. Those neighbors sent their children to let other neighbors know. We had it organized. We were prepared. Everybody who was willing and able to do so went to the boy's cottage before the knights got there. The neighbors brought with them whatever they had, mostly pitchforks, to fight off the knights. They all wore bags over their heads with holes cut out for their eyes. They looked like highwaymen. Then they hid themselves behind bushes and trees around the boy's home. It wasn't hard for them to do that. The abducting knights never came during the day."

"Were you with the neighbors?"

Ophelia looked at her family. The horse was pulling the load of hay on the lane through the pasture to their gray, weathered-wood barn. Ophelia's older daughter led the horse. Her other children and her husband followed the wagon.

Ophelia's Story: Twelve Years before the Visit

"Stop where you are!" Ophelia yelled.

The abducting knights had reached the front door to the cottage the youth and his family lived in.

Ophelia's command was also the signal for the neighbors to light their torches and reveal themselves, their weaponry, their numbers, their fearlessness.

The captain of the knights turned to look. "What the fuck is this?" he asked.

"You have two choices," Ophelia shouted from her position among the neighbors. "You can go away and leave the boy you've come for. Or you can die."

The knights had tumbled into a world whose existence they'd never imagined. Common people were challenging them.

"We'll kill you and celebrate," Ophelia said, stepping forward, brandishing her pitchfork. "We'll show the king and lord chamberlain what we can do. We'll dig graves for you in the forest. We'll dance on them. We've got fiddlers and flutists with us. They'd love to watch us skipping to their beat, celebrating your horrific deaths."

Several of the musicians offered a brief sample of what they'd play. It was a familiar dirge speeded up for sprightly dancing.

The knights remained frozen at the cottage door. They were apparently unable to believe they hadn't taken leave of their senses, imagining voices and visions the way people who'd lost their minds did.

"It's time for you to go now," Ophelia said. "I'll count. When I reach the number three, I'll give the order for your slaughter. Your blood will turn the ground you stand on crimson."

"Save your breath, you damned witch," the captain, wise enough to know defeat when he saw it, yelled back at her. "We'll go."

The Visit

"My father told me," Ophelia said, "when you threaten to kill people, you need to make them think nothing could give you more pleasure than their death. I don't know how he knew that, but it seemed to work."

"Did your father discover what you'd done?" Fortinbras asked.

Ophelia laughed. "He and the royal family found out that same night what the people had done. They didn't know what I'd done, though. Horatio and I were wearing the farmers' clothes we always wore here. We had bags over our heads. The few neighbors who knew I was the lord chamberlain's daughter promised us they'd tell no one else. They kept their word. We knew we could trust them. They'd either lost sons in the war or were in danger of losing them. They despised my father and the king."

"Did you take part in the resistance after that?"

"Horatio and I went to every village where a youth was about to turn seventeen. They'd all stopped volunteering. We joined the boy's neighbors when they confronted the abducting knights. We watched the knights ride off empty-handed time after time. We even took part in the confrontations at Elsinore Castle. The resisting servants didn't want to be identified and punished later. So they also wore bags over their heads. Horatio and I wore servants' clothes and brandished butcher knives, axes or whatever else we could get our hands on. We looked up at the castle balcony where my father, the king, the queen and Prince Claudius stood, safely above the angry crowd. They screamed down at us. They promised hangings for traitors. The next day the castle servants went back to work as if nothing had happened. They assured the royal family and my father they'd been nowhere near the previous night's mob. Nor did they know any other servants who'd taken part in the disturbance. The persons with bags over their heads must've come in from nearby villages and dressed themselves to look like servants. Everybody knew farmers were the rebellious sort, always ready for an excuse to commit treason. They weren't loyal to their betters the way servants were."

Fortinbras laughed.

One of the servants in the mobs at Elsinore Castle was the person who'd recently told Fortinbras the lord chamberlain's daughter was still alive. The servant had done it at Ophelia's request.

Ophelia's Story: Twelve Years before the Visit

From his allowance as a prince, Hamlet paid the expenses for Horatio to visit him in Wittenberg. Horatio soon discovered Hamlet had little desire either to learn German or to attend his classes at the university. He spent most of his waking hours drinking.

Hamlet took Horatio to a beer garden, then with leaves turning yellow, popular among his classmates. After they received their second steins, Hamlet had a question for his guest.

He knew Horatio and Ophelia had learned to speak German when they were still quite young. They'd befriended several of the daughters and sons of the servants of the diplomats from the German-speaking principalities who came to see the king and lord chamberlain at Elsinore Castle. The royal tutor had told them hosts could always make a good impression on their visitors from foreign lands by speaking their language.

Hamlet gestured toward his classmates. "What are they saying about me? What do they think is so fucking amusing?"

The classmates were in fact talking about Hamlet and laughing.

Horatio found it difficult to respond. "They say," he decided to reply, "your father, the king of Denmark, sent you out of your country to save you from fighting in the war he started with the Norwegians."

"That isn't funny," Hamlet said. "Not even slightly. What else are they saying?"

"They say your father kept you out of the war because you'd probably end up dead in it."

"Do you find that laughable?"

"Of course not."

"Go on then. Those assholes are saying a lot more than that."

"Yes, they are."

"Then tell me what it is."

Horatio took a deep breath. "They're saying your father's war with the Norwegians was stupid to begin with, and it's utterly hopeless now. But he and his idiotic lord chamberlain are stuck with it. They can't win it, and they can't end it. It's more proof, your classmates say, if anybody needs it, those ignorant Scandinavians will never amount to anything."

Hamlet couldn't take his eyes off his amused classmates.

"I'm very sorry," Horatio said, "they find somebody else's woe so entertaining."

"I'm not," Hamlet said, motioning to the waiter to bring him and his guest their third steins of beer. "If I were in their shoes, I'd be laughing myself."

The Visit

"I'm curious about something," Fortinbras said. "Did you and Horatio speak about his conversations with Hamlet in Wittenberg before and after they happened?"

"We did," Ophelia replied.

"Did you go over beforehand what they'd talk about?"

"We did."

"After Horatio's visit, did you speak with him about what he and Hamlet actually said?"

"We did, down to the very last detail."

Fortinbras glanced at Ophelia's family.

The older daughter led the horse pulling the wagon up an earthen ramp into the second story of the barn. She and her father and brothers would fork the new hay into the haymows on either side of the wagon. When winter came again, Ophelia and her family would fork the hay down chutes to the first floor of the barn. The cattle, sheep and goats would feed on it there, sheltered from the cold, snow, ice and wind.

"Did Horatio tell Hamlet," Fortinbras asked, "you and he were taking part in the resistance?"

"No," Ophelia replied. "Horatio didn't say a word about that. Some of the lords were sending their sons to see the prince in Wittenberg. We didn't want Hamlet to get drunk with them and start babbling about what we were doing."

"Did Hamlet ask Horatio about you?"

"He asked about me. Horatio told him I was lonely in the castle. He said I missed him and my brother and the good times the four of us used to enjoy together, but what could I do about it? We'd simply outgrown our youth."

"Did Horatio tell Hamlet he was living and working here on your aunt's farm?"

"No. Horatio told Hamlet he was still working in the royal stable."

Ophelia glanced again at the barn, which was on the far side of her family's vegetable garden and vineyard. Their cottage, with its stone walls and chimney, mullioned windows and thatched roof, was on the near side. Red roses and white daisies surrounded their home as if it were in a bouquet.

"Horatio and I," she said, "had learned we needed to tell falsehoods more often that we told the truth. But we'd also discovered invented stories were far more difficult to remember than true stories. So we rehearsed our lies, over and over again, before we told them. We also repeated them, endlessly, after we told them. In those days, for us, lying became an art."

Chapter Five

Ophelia's Story: Eleven Years before the Visit

After Laertes found out Horatio had visited Hamlet in Wittenberg, he paid money from his allowance for Horatio to see him in France.

Growing up with the three of them, Ophelia was amused that both Laertes, the lord chamberlain's son, and Hamlet, the prince, claimed they were the best friend of Horatio, a boy who seemed destined to spend his life working in the royal stable.

Soon after Horatio arrived in Paris, he learned Laertes had no more interest than the prince in learning a foreign language or attending classes at the university he was enrolled in. Unlike Hamlet, though, Laertes did his drinking by himself, in the garret he'd rented.

All day—*toute la journée*—his landlady confided when she let Horatio in and directed him to the stairway to the upper floors of her house.

Horatio and Ophelia had learned to speak, read and write French the same way they'd learned German, Norwegian, Swedish, Dutch and English.

Laertes poured wine into goblets for his guest and himself.

"It comes from Bordeaux," he said, "wherever in hell that is."

Horatio and Ophelia had seen where it was on dusty maps they'd found in the royal library in Elsinore Castle. Whether it was in hell or heaven or somewhere in between, kings and dukes, even Roman legions, had fought wars over it.

Laertes and Horatio drank their claret in comfortable chairs with a low table in front of them. Through two dormer windows, they had a view of boats sailing on the Seine.

Laertes seemed eager to let Horatio know the lords' sons who'd paid visits to the prince in Wittenberg had also come to see the lord chamberlain's son in France.

Laertes peered over the rim of his goblet at Horatio. "Our dear friend Prince Hamlet will soon find out what we've been up to."

"What might that be?" Horatio asked.

"The most powerful lords in Denmark, Prince Claudius and I have formed an alliance."

Assuming he'd already imbibed an excessive amount of what Laertes had told him was the finest wine France had to offer, Horatio set his goblet down on the table at his knee.

"Hamlet's uncle, the great lords and you?" he asked.

Laertes nodded. "We've decided Denmark's line of succession badly needs amending."

"In what way?"

"We've agreed eighteen-year-old Hamlet might be legally old enough to serve as king if anything happened to his father, but he's damned well not fit to perform the duties of a king."

Horatio made no attempt to conceal his surprise. "Why do you think Prince Hamlet isn't fit to be the king?"

Laertes sighed. "You and I might be the best friends the prince will ever have, but we've got to face the facts. Hamlet can no longer control his tongue. He tells the lords' sons what he told you. The war with Norway, he says, is hopeless. It was a tragic error for his father and my father to begin it in the first place."

Horatio gave up on the boats floating on the Seine and looked at his host. "Don't you agree with the prince? Don't you agree the war was a stupid damned mistake from the start? Don't you agree Denmark can never gain anything from it?"

"Of course, I agree with all that. But the prince can't say those things to the lords' sons. The lords have lost a great number of their knights and cartloads of treasure fighting that war. The prince can't tell them it's hopeless to continue fighting it. He can't tell them they threw away all those knights and all that treasure for nothing. Not if he expects to become the king of Denmark some day."

"He can't tell them the truth? He can't tell them any king in his right mind would stop the war this moment and cut his people's losses?"

Laertes chose to wax indignant. "No, the prince can't do that. He has to give the lords hope we can turn the war around, beat that fucking Norwegian prince on the field of battle, bring him in chains to Elsinore Castle and chop off his damned head."

"So how," Horatio asked, as if he hadn't already guessed, "do you propose amending the line of succession?"

"Prince Claudius will be first in our new line. Prince Hamlet will be second."

"Prince Claudius and the lords will ask the king to demote his son in favor of his brother?"

"The king has already agreed to do it. So has my father. They'll use the demotion to force Prince Hamlet into supporting the war. If he wants to be the first in the line to the throne again, he'll tell the people what a prince needs to tell them."

"What about Prince Fortinbras? Will he still be third in the line of succession?"

Laertes laughed. "Only for now. Only until we separate his head from the rest of his body on the executioner's block at Elsinore Castle. I'm told people find him easy on their eyes. I wonder what they'll think of him when he's headless and covered with blood. After that, I can promise you, he won't be in anybody's line of succession for anything."

The Visit

Ophelia wondered if her guest's grimace arose from the thought of an executioner's blade slicing through his neck.

In any event, Fortinbras had more questions for her. "Did you and Horatio speak about his conversations with Laertes in France before and after they occurred?"

"We did," Ophelia replied.

"Did Horatio tell Laertes he'd left the royal stable? Did he tell him he'd taken up farming and the study of plants and mushrooms?"

Ophelia shook her head. "My brother was just as capable as Prince Hamlet of babbling over his beverage—and revealing information to lords' sons they had no need to know."

"That makes sense," Fortinbras agreed. "I don't understand, though, the intensity of your brother's animosity toward Prince Hamlet. Not to the point where he'd plot to demote his childhood friend in the line of succession—and in favor of the odious Uncle Claudius, of all people."

"Laertes was his father's son. He wished to rule the kingdom from behind the throne the way any self-respecting lord chamberlain would."

"He didn't think Prince Hamlet would go along with that?"

"He knew damned well Hamlet wouldn't. Our father had convinced the king and the queen he knew how to win the war with Norway, but he obviously didn't. Time and again, Hamlet told us he didn't want a pushy but ineffectual lord chamberlain like my father when he became king. In fact, no lord chamberlain would ever tell him what to do."

"Even when you were children, Hamlet spoke this way?"

Ophelia nodded. "On the surface of things, he and my brother were best friends. Almost everybody thought they were. But as they grew up, they actually became rivals, bitter rivals. When they played games, they did everything they could to outdo the other, whatever the game was. Hamlet thought the king should be on top. My brother thought that position belonged to the lord chamberlain. They never could've ruled the kingdom together. Horatio and I could see how hopeless it would've been. Hamlet and Laertes saw it themselves."

"Is that why your brother opposed your marriage to Hamlet?"

Ophelia shrugged. "It could've been one of his reasons. I'm certain he didn't want Hamlet and me united in our opposition to him. He knew he'd end up with no power whatsoever. He'd be a figurehead lord chamberlain."

Ophelia's Story: Eleven Years before the Visit

Polonius summoned Ophelia to his chamber and told her the king had decided to send Horatio to Wittenberg to inform Prince Hamlet he'd been demoted in the line of succession.

"I'll have someone take a message to Horatio," Ophelia said. "I know you don't want me speaking to him myself."

Polonius shook his head. "I want you to speak to him yourself. He can keep a secret, can't he?"

"He certainly can."

"We don't want the servants and the people talking about this before the prince knows what the king's decided to do."

"Horatio is the most discreet person I've ever met."

Polonius removed a purse from his coat pocket and handed it to Ophelia. "This is more than enough money for that stable boy to pay for his transportation and lodging. You can even use some of it to buy clothes for him so he looks like a proper lord's son. We don't want a prince of Denmark appearing to entertain a servant. Those damned Germans will jump at any chance they can get to laugh at us."

Ophelia's Story: Eleven Years before the Visit

Hamlet took Horatio back to the beer garden he and his classmates favored. He was damned glad, he said, the spring day was warm enough for them to do their drinking outside.

Early on during their first stein of beer, Hamlet wrinkled his brow. "They want me to tell the lords' sons I'm all in favor of their stupid war?"

Horatio nodded. "That's what Ophelia's father says you have to do—if you want to regain your rightful position in the line of succession."

The classmates had a youth with them who wasn't dressed the way they were. Horatio guessed he was a servant. The classmates were buying him beer. Then Horatio realized why. The servant could speak Danish as well as German. He paid close attention to whatever Hamlet and Horatio said. Then he repeated their conversation, in German, for the classmates. Horatio wondered if he was from a border area where the people spoke both languages.

"What if I say," Hamlet asked, "fuck my position in the line of succession? Who in their right mind would want to be the king of a country as desperate as Denmark anyway?"

As the classmates laughed, Horatio placed his stein of beer on the table. "I couldn't agree with you more," he said, glancing at the interpreter. "I'd much rather tend horses."

"I mean," Hamlet said, "the war was a stupid fucking mistake from the day my father started it. Far too many people on both sides have wasted their lives in it. Nobody can justify all the death and destruction it's caused. The only right thing to do now is to end the war. Does Denmark still hold any territories it didn't have before the war began?"

"Everybody I've talked with at Elsinore says Fortinbras has retaken almost all the land our army won."

"Then we should end the war and hope Fortinbras doesn't attempt to take any land away from us for punishment. But nobody in Denmark can want the war to continue. We have to admit it's hopeless. How can my father and Polonius expect me to say anything different to the lords' sons? I'd be lying through my teeth."

Horatio shook his head. "I wouldn't want to be in a position where I had to do that."

Hamlet ordered another stein of beer for both of them.

"But I'm worried about Ophelia," he said.

Horatio had wondered when the discussion of Hamlet's place in the line of succession would go where it had to go. "Why are you worried about her?"

"If she can't look forward to me becoming the king when my father dies, why would she want to marry me?"

"I thought you said she told you she doesn't want to marry you."

"That's what she told me. That isn't what she meant. I could tell. She was trying to pacify her brother. *He* doesn't want us to marry. We'd both outrank him. His sister and I could tell him to go fuck himself whenever we pleased. He'd be a nobody to us."

"Wouldn't you make him your lord chamberlain?"

"Of course I would. And I've told him, more than a few times, I would. He wouldn't be satisfied with that, though. He wants me to marry a woman he could manipulate. He sure as hell knows he could never manipulate Ophelia. She has a mind of her own. You've seen it as much as I have. Nobody will ever manipulate her. Sometimes I think that's why I'm in love with her."

"And you think she loves you?"

"I know she does. If her brother wasn't being such an asshole about it, she'd tell me she loves me. She'd tell me she wants to marry me more than she wants anything else."

Hamlet lifted his second stein of beer to his lips and took a long drink from it.

"Damn it all to hell," he said, setting the stein on the table between him and Horatio. "I suppose I've got to do what my father and her father want me to do."

"What are you saying?"

"I've got to tell those lords' sons I support my father's fucked-up war. Hell, I'll tell them I hope it goes on forever if that's what it takes to make Denmark whole again."

Horatio, hearing the classmates gasp after their interpreter repeated those remarks in German, also took a long drink from his stein.

"You'll do that," he asked Hamlet, "to convince Ophelia to marry you?"

"I told you, I'm in love with her. She's the only woman I want to marry. And she isn't going to marry a prince who's going nowhere. Not her. I'd be as much use to her as a footman. No, she'll only marry a prince who stands to become the king the moment his father takes his last breath."

Hamlet downed more beer.

"Fuck that damned war!" he said. "Fuck those Norwegians! Fuck Prince Fortinbras! Fuck those people resisting the war! Who in hell do they think they are anyway? Death to the traitors, I say!"

Hamlet was loud enough to be heard from one end of the beer garden to the other. The classmates weren't the only customers gesturing toward Hamlet with their steins and laughing.

Chapter Six

Ophelia's Story: Ten Years before the Visit

"Your Majesties," Polonius said, "I have some very unpleasant news."

He stood before the throne speaking to the king, queen and Prince Claudius in a session of the king's court closed to the public. As the bride-to-be of Prince Hamlet, though, Ophelia could and did attend such proceedings.

"Those damned Norwegians," her father said, "have forced us out."

"What do you mean," Queen Gertrude asked, with more than a hint of ire in her voice, "they've forced us out?"

Polonius cowered. "Our army has given up all the territories it won."

Claudius snickered. "Your army needed many more years to win those territories than it did to lose them."

The king ignored his younger brother and turned to the lord chamberlain. "Where is our army now?"

"On the sea, Your Highness," Polonius replied, "coming home."

Ophelia had heard rumors the army was retreating across the sea in the ships it had used for the invasion that began the war. The vessels were headed, word had it, to the ports from which Denmark had launched its assault on its neighbor. If so, its army would be right back where it started.

"All for nothing!" she heard people say, some muttering the words under their breath, others shouting them from their windows to their neighbors.

"What are your plans for our army," the king asked Polonius, "after it comes home?"

The lord chamberlain took a deep breath. "I've given orders to the commanders to remain on our seacoast closest to Norway and regroup."

"Regroup?" Claudius asked. "For what purpose?"

"For the defense of our homeland," Polonius replied.

"What do you mean?" the queen asked. "Do you think the Norwegian prince intends to invade our territories?"

Polonius nodded. "I have no doubt he does. I've heard he's provisioning ships in the same ports where ours so recently stood at anchor. What can be the point of that but to bring the war home to us?"

"He seeks revenge," the king said, his baritone voice as filled with doom as Ophelia had ever heard it.

"Precisely," Polonius agreed.

Claudius shook his head. "I think we should change the purpose of our regrouping to something nobler than fending off Fortinbras."

"What do you mean?" Polonius asked.

"I mean," Claudius said, "our purpose should be to nip his invasion plans in the bud."

"And how, my dear prince," Gertrude asked, in the tone of voice she reserved for him, "do you propose to do that nipping in the bud?"

"By taking the war back to him," Claudius replied.

"By invading Norway again?" Polonius snapped.

"He'll never expect it," Claudius said. "We'll catch him totally unawares. His army will fall to pieces."

The king scoffed. "The same army that just now forced our army to flee Norway?"

"With all due respect, Your Majesty," Claudius replied, "you may have lost hope for your army, but I believe it can prevail. I believe, properly led, it can restore to us the lands the Norwegian kings stole long ago. I believe the war must go on until we win it, wholly win it. We must leave no further doubt in anybody's mind that whatever belongs to a king of Denmark is in fact under his rule."

Polonius turned to the king. "I have no quarrel with the prince when he says we must fight the war until we win it, completely win it, leaving no Danish territory under the dominium of a Norwegian king. I disagree with your brother, though, in his tactics. I believe we should let young Prince Fortinbras attempt to invade us. After we hold him off, after we reduce his army to piles of decomposing bodies on our beaches, after we burn his ships, then we should chase his ass back to Norway, resume the offensive, retake the territories his father illegally rules and make Denmark whole again."

The king nodded. "I've heard enough."

"That's enough?" Claudius asked, knowing he wouldn't win the argument. "A strategy with no surprise in it is enough?"

The king once again ignored his brother. "Lord chamberlain, please order our army to prepare to defend our land from the Norwegian prince's invasion."

Gertrude's servants had told Ophelia a story. When the king and lord chamberlain were still planning the war, the queen had argued the king should personally lead the invasion of Norway. The forty-one-year-old king, though, claimed he was too old to perform such an arduous task.

Gertrude had known, her servants said, the king would never agree to lead the army himself. But his refusal gave her the chance to put forward her first choice to lead the invasion, the king's twenty-two-year-old brother. Unfortunately for the queen, the king rejected Claudius's nomination as quickly and firmly as he had his own.

Gertrude told her servants the jealous king didn't want to give his brother what she believed would be a golden opportunity for him to cover himself with military glory. She would've accompanied the army in their boats, she said. She would've ridden her horse to its battles. She would've watched the youthful prince personally kill Norwegians. She would've toasted him at the victory celebrations as the hero he was meant to be.

The servants came to the end of their story laughing. The queen, they told Ophelia, was the only person in Elsinore Castle who didn't know by then Claudius hadn't the slightest desire to take part in a military battle, either in Norway or any other land.

The Visit

"You were a spy," Fortinbras said. "You used your position as Hamlet's bride-to-be to spy on your father and the royal family."

Ophelia nodded. "You can say that."

"You must've told them you'd marry Hamlet."

"I'd told them I'd marry him. And why not? They'd given me no choice in the matter. I was the lord chamberlain's daughter. I'd be Prince Hamlet's bride whether I wanted to be or not. So I told them I'd changed my mind. I'd gladly become his bride. I knew what I was doing. I took what they gave me. They only had themselves to blame for what I did with it."

Ophelia's Story: Ten Years before the Visit

In order to avoid being seen, Ophelia and Horatio arrived at the rear entrance to the Swedish ambassador's residence well before dawn. Soon afterward, they and she rode off together in her carriage. They kept the window curtains closed.

Ophelia and Horatio sat on the front seat, facing backward.

The ambassador, Christina, sat alone on the rear seat, facing them. She was only a few years older than they were. Polonius had said she was the Swedish queen's niece. But Ophelia had learned she was, more specifically, the elderly monarch's grandniece. The queen had recently appointed her to her position in Denmark.

"Forgive me for being so blunt," Christina said, speaking in Swedish as Ophelia had requested, "but I must tell you Her Majesty detests your country's war with Norway. A war between neighbors, she says, is almost always a disaster for our country. And this war, she made certain I understood, has disrupted trading to and from Sweden to an intolerable degree and for an unbearable length of time. She insisted I should try anything I could to bring the war to an end."

Ophelia looked at Christina intently. "And that's why you're taking us to Norway."

Christina, who wore her blond hair surprisingly short, nodded. "The queen knows what we're doing."

Ophelia's Story: Ten Years before the Visit

That evening they had to travel through a Danish army encampment before they could reach the port they were headed to.

When they stopped at the guard post, Christina opened her window curtain only enough to show the sentry her credentials, which bore the queen of Sweden's seal.

She nodded toward Ophelia and Horatio, who remained out of the direct light from the sentry's torch.

"These are my servants," Christina said. "I received permission from the lord chamberlain to bring two with me."

The sentry waved them on.

The port was a short distance away.

Ophelia and Horatio slept that moonlit night in the captain's guestroom in a Swedish merchant vessel traveling otherwise empty to Norway. They'd previously sailed in fishing boats on the coastal waters of Denmark but never in a ship on the high seas.

After they disembarked the next morning, a Norwegian knight rode with them in a carriage to one of the larger tents in the Norwegian army's encampment. The knight took them inside it and, calling them "the Danish lord chamberlain's daughter Ophelia and her aide Horatio," introduced them to Prince Fortinbras.

Ophelia's Story: Ten Years before the Visit

The prince and his two guests sat at a round table. They were the only persons present in the royal headquarters tent for the Norwegian army. Ophelia noted it was as sparely furnished as her aunt's farmhouse.

Fortinbras sat with his hands clasped together on the table in front of him as if he wished to emphasize he wasn't armed or ready for battle.

"I understand you have a request for me," he said, speaking in Norwegian as Ophelia had suggested they do. "Based upon what the Swedish ambassador to Denmark has told me, I'm eager to know what your request is."

"I came here to implore you," Ophelia said, "not to invade Denmark."

The prince seemed surprised. Ophelia couldn't tell whether he was reacting to her request itself or the direct manner in which she'd stated it.

He thought for a few moments before he spoke. "I wish I could grant your request. This war has killed and injured far too many people on both sides already. And all for nothing, my people say."

Ophelia nodded. "All for nothing—that's what many of our people say."

There was a second, larger table in the tent. Ophelia had noticed, as the knight led her and Horatio past it to meet the prince, a number of maps lay open on it like secrets revealed. They were maps of Denmark.

Fortinbras took his time before he spoke. "But if I don't invade your country and destroy your army, what will stop your king from using it to invade my country again? What will stop him from beginning a second phase of the war as deadly and pointless as the first?"

"I hope," Ophelia replied, "our king and my father realize you've already destroyed their army. I hope they understand it's no longer fit to fight a war—and it won't be fit to fight a war again for at least another generation."

"On our way here," Horatio chose to say, "we saw one of our army's encampments. The knights were wearing rags. Many of them appeared to be emaciated, as if they might soon starve to death. I can't imagine they'd wish to resume the fighting."

The prince nodded. "Sometimes, though, kings and lord chamberlains miscalculate. They fail to see—or refuse to see—what reasonable people see."

Ophelia shook her head. "But suppose our king and my father did miscalculate. Suppose they did restart their foolish war. You could very well end up glad they did. You could more easily resist another invasion of Norway than mount an offensive struggle in Denmark. You could let our king and my father utterly destroy their army all by themselves. They'd relieve you of the need to launch a costly invasion across the sea to do it."

Fortinbras chose not to respond to those remarks.

"You could become the king of Denmark someday," Ophelia said. "Your reign, unlike the present king's, could be a great success. History could view it kindly."

Fortinbras shook his head. "I have no wish to be the king of Denmark. Taking my father's place here in Norway, when the time comes, will be a burden heavy enough for my shoulders."

"Many Danes, though," Ophelia said, "might view the matter differently."

She once again appeared to have caught the prince off guard.

He removed his hands from the table and grasped the arms of his chair. "Can you tell me why you say that?"

"Most of Denmark," Ophelia replied, "might be happy to have your shoulders bearing the burden of being their king. And they might wish to help ease the burden on you as much as they could. Especially if you spared them the death and destruction an invasion on their soil would bring."

From where she sat, she would've said the prince's shoulders looked fit enough to bear the heaviest burdens. Christina had told her and Horatio the prince had personally fought in every major battle in the war.

"I understand," Fortinbras said, "I'm third in the line of succession to Denmark's throne. I also understand you're betrothed to one of the two princes who rank above me in that line."

Ophelia glanced at Horatio and laughed before she turned to

Fortinbras again. "The present king of Denmark and my father believe I'll marry Prince Hamlet. So does he."

"But you don't intend to become his bride?"

"I intend to fight becoming his bride in every way I can. I liken myself to a Norwegian fending off a ruthless invader."

Fortinbras stared at Ophelia. "You have no wish to see Prince Hamlet become Denmark's king?"

Ophelia sighed. "I'm afraid any reign of his would be as disastrous as his father's has proved to be. His uncle, despite his status as Queen Gertrude's favorite, offers even less hope. No, I believe the best king for the Danes would be you."

Fortinbras couldn't take his eyes off Ophelia. "I can't promise you I won't invade your country."

"I wouldn't ask you to do that," Ophelia said

"I do value, though," Fortinbras said, "what you've told me. It'll weigh heavily in whatever I decide to do."

Ophelia nodded. "You've given me all I came here for. I'd like to mention one more thing, though, if I might."

"Of course," Fortinbras said.

"I don't blame you," she said, "for worrying about the burden of being a king. Anybody who wanted to be a good king could only be very worried. But if that person didn't have to be concerned about another invasion from a hostile neighboring country, the burden would be a lot less."

"It would," Fortinbras agreed.

"And I can't imagine," Ophelia said, "two countries sharing a king would go to war, or continue a war, with one another."

Fortinbras laughed. "No, that wouldn't seem likely."

Chapter Seven

The Visit

"I have to admit," Fortinbras said, "I had a difficult time convincing the Norwegian lords we should stay put in Norway."

"They had other ideas?" Ophelia asked.

"They knew our army had broken your army. They wanted me to sail across the sea and attack what was left of it in Denmark."

"To make certain they wouldn't have to fight the evil Danes again for another generation—or two or three?"

Fortinbras nodded. "For that. Also for revenge. Mainly, though, to occupy as much of Denmark as they could."

"What did they plan to do with the Danes living in the parts of Denmark they occupied?"

"They would've chased them out."

"And replaced them with Norwegians?"

"That's what they wanted to do."

"They would've made the Danes hate you."

"They told me the Danes already hated me. I'd defeated them. I couldn't make matters any worse by taking a large part of Denmark and giving it to my Norwegians."

"And the Norwegians you would've given most of that land to would've been your lords?"

"Of course. That was their plan."

Ophelia's Story: Ten Years before the Visit

Christina was waiting in her carriage for Ophelia and Horatio when their ship returned to the Danish port from which it had sailed for Norway.

Despite the lateness of the hour, the ambassador was as effusive as she'd been during their previous carriage ride.

At one point she looked at Ophelia and sighed. "I spoke with your father. He told me he and your king don't give a damn how much my aunt complains about their war with Norway. He even warned me they might start another war. He said it would be a war she'd find even more objectionable than she does the current one."

"Another war?" Ophelia asked.

Christina nodded. "Your father told me he and your king would begin the war by invading Sweden."

"Sweden?" Horatio asked. "Why on earth would they invade Sweden?"

Christina sighed again. "I asked the lord chamberlain that question. He gave me the same argument he'd given the Norwegians. He said he can prove a large part of present-day Sweden used to belong to Denmark. He told me the Danish king has every right to extend his rule to those territories. If it takes a war to accomplish that, he said, so be it."

Ophelia's Story: Ten Years before the Visit

The day after Ophelia returned from Norway, she was with her father, the king, the queen and Claudius in the odious uncle's chamber in Elsinore Castle. They'd gathered to celebrate his birthday. They sat on the colorful silk couches he'd purchased during his last visit to Italy. They drank the claret he'd brought home from France.

"I have some news," Polonius said. "It's on very good authority."

"What's the news?" the king asked.

The solemnity Ophelia heard in the king's voice and saw on his face led her to believe he didn't expect the news to lift his spirits.

"Just as I thought," Polonius replied, "that arrogant Norwegian prince is preparing to invade Denmark."

"And who," the queen asked the lord chamberlain, "is your very good authority?"

"The Swedish ambassador," Polonius replied.

Gertrude scoffed. "That pretty girl the men can't take their eyes off?"

Polonius laughed. "She's the one."

Gertrude closed her eyes and slowly shook her head. "The queen of Sweden appointed her silly niece to be her ambassador to Elsinore Castle for one reason only."

"What was her reason?" Ophelia asked.

Gertrude gave the lord chamberlain's daughter a sour look. "To let us know what low regard she has for Denmark. The first time I saw that niece, with her short hair, I thought she was a boy, maybe the son of the real ambassador. To tell you the truth, I beg to differ with your father. I wouldn't consider her good authority for anything she told me."

Polonius glared at Gertrude. "I've learned this niece of the queen of Sweden is especially close to that Norwegian prince we've been fighting. They're distant cousins, you know, on his father's side."

"Thank goodness," Gertrude said, "she's not related to us."

Claudius turned to his brother. "No matter what the ambassador said, I'm certain Fortinbras intends to invade Denmark. And that means we need to attack his army first. There they'll be, loading their ships in their ports. And we'll sweep down on them, from out of nowhere, and sink those ships. We won't just put to an end that prince's dream of conquering Denmark. We'll go on and totally win the war we should've won years ago."

Queen Gertrude carefully listened to every word Claudius spoke. Then she nodded and beamed her approval.

Polonius, on the other hand, looked at the prince without concealing his contempt. "What makes you think we can sweep down on our enemy from out of nowhere? Do you possess some magical power that will enable our ships to sail across the sea invisible to Norwegian eyes?"

Once again, the king chose to ignore his brother. "We'll need to stick to our plan and prepare to defend ourselves against the invasion Prince Fortinbras obviously has in store for us."

Claudius scoffed. "An outright surrender would be better than that plan. It would at least be honest."

The queen laughed. She enjoyed her brother-in-law's insolence as much as he did.

The Visit

Fortinbras looked as if he were a child who'd wandered into a dark woods and gotten lost. "I have to admit," he said, "I don't understand Claudius. Did he really think the defeated Danish army could immediately invade Norway again?"

"I'm certain," Ophelia replied, "he didn't give a damn whether it could or couldn't. He made his argument for the attention it got him. He wanted the people to think he had more confidence in the Danish army than his brother the king did. He knew what he was doing."

Ron Fritsch

Ophelia's Story: Ten Years before the Visit

Gertrude turned to Ophelia. "Maybe we should dispatch that young man from the stable to be our ambassador to Sweden. I'd say he's just as pretty as their queen's niece. Wouldn't you agree?"

In the long silence that followed the queen's insinuating remarks and question, the king drank the last of his wine, placed the empty goblet on the table next to him and began gurgling.

He got up from the couch he'd been sitting on and stumbled. He moaned and grasped his midsection with his hands as if he'd taken a sword in his gut. He vomited some of the wine he'd been drinking. He fell to the floor.

Claudius and his other guests rose to their feet as if protocol required they stand during a royal assassination attempt.

The king writhed on the carpet for a moment or two before he went motionless.

Polonius knelt beside him. He placed his fingers on the king's wrist and neck feeling for a pulse. He listened at the king's nose and mouth for any indication he was still breathing.

Polonius looked up at Claudius, Gertrude and Ophelia and shook his head.

The Visit

"The king had been poisoned," Fortinbras said.

Ophelia nodded. "We assumed that was the case from the moment he stumbled and fell."

"And Claudius was considered the culprit because he was the host, and the king was drinking his wine?"

Ophelia shook her head. "It wasn't just that. Something very peculiar happened shortly before the king died. It involved the servant, Eric, who'd worked for Claudius the longest, the one who handled his most personal matters. He appeared in the parlor where we were talking and drinking. He went directly to the king and asked if he wanted another goblet of wine. He didn't ask anybody else. I was sitting near the king, and my goblet was also empty. Eric had to have seen it was. But he didn't ask me if I wanted more wine. The king acknowledged he'd like another goblet, and Eric brought it to him, a single goblet on a tray that easily could've held half a dozen. After what happened, it seemed to me, and still does, Eric wanted to make certain he gave a tainted goblet of wine to the king and only the king."

Ophelia could tell Fortinbras was still lost in the woods.

"So Claudius," he said, "made no attempt to conceal his identity as his brother's assassin. He left it all too obvious he committed the murder. His most loyal servant gave the king the goblet of wine laced with the poison that killed him. And Claudius knew he'd become the king the moment his brother died. Talk about having both a great opportunity and a powerful motive to commit a murder."

Ophelia shrugged. "The people decided Claudius brazenly, shamelessly murdered his brother. But he'd never given a damn what the people thought of him. Why should his brother's assassination make him change his mind about that?"

Ophelia's Story: Ten Years before the Visit

The queen looked at the king, lying immobile on the floor, as if she'd happened upon the corpse of a stranger.

She turned to Claudius, who embraced her.

"Dear, dear Gertrude," he said.

Polonius rose to his feet. "We'll need to tell the people he was gravely ill."

"Should we carry him to his bedroom?" Gertrude asked. "It might be better if we told the people he died there."

Polonius shook his head. "The servants saw him here, drinking with us. You know how they like to make up wild stories about the royal family. Then they repeat them as if they're the absolute truth. And the people always love to hear about the latest shenanigans in Elsinore Castle."

Claudius nodded. "But we can still tell the people he was dreadfully ill. We can say we didn't inform the servants because we knew they couldn't, and wouldn't, do anything to help him."

The queen, still embracing the new king, also nodded. "Maybe we can find a doctor who'll agree with us the poor man was hopelessly ill."

The lord chamberlain smirked. "A small amount of money should take care of that."

Ron Fritsch

The Visit

"You mean to tell me," Fortinbras asked, "Claudius made no attempt to deny he'd murdered his brother?"

Ophelia shrugged again. "How could he? He'd either ordered Eric to poison the king's wine, or Eric had done it on his own. Or maybe it was something in between. Maybe Claudius had whispered in Eric's ear how much he wanted to be rid of his brother. In any event, once Claudius became the king, he wasn't going to accuse his own most loyal servant of killing the old king. How would that look? No, once the assassination was an accomplished fact, however it happened, Claudius, the beneficiary of it, was stuck with it."

"And Queen Gertrude and your father immediately assumed Claudius had murdered the king?"

"What else could they assume? They'd seen what I'd seen. They'd seen what Eric had done. They chose not to speak of it openly. I made the same choice. I had no wish to accuse Eric of assassinating the king. More probably than not, he was only following the orders Claudius, the true assassin, had given him. I assume others who later heard whispered accounts of the incident drew the same conclusion I did. If anybody should be punished for the assassination of the king, that person was Claudius—not the loyal, hard-working servant everybody loved."

"And the queen and your father were perfectly willing to help Claudius cover up his hideous crime?"

Fortinbras had led the Norwegian army to a total victory over the villainous invading Danes, and yet he sometimes seemed to Ophelia more like an innocent child than a conquering hero. She imagined him in the pasture with her children, frolicking with the calves, lambs and kids.

"What else could Gertrude and my father do?" Ophelia asked. "The old king lay dead on his brother's imported carpet. Claudius was the new king. My father wished to remain the lord chamberlain, no matter who the king was. Gertrude wished to remain the queen, especially if the king was Claudius."

Fortinbras blinked his eyes. "And none of them—Claudius, Gertrude, your father—had any objection to your seeing and hearing everything they said and did?"

"Why would they? I'm sure they didn't imagine I had any wish to accuse them of committing crimes. They must've thought, with good reason, I wanted my father to retain his lofty position. If he didn't, I couldn't continue being the lord chamberlain's daughter. And I'd told them I looked forward to becoming Prince Hamlet's bride—and, someday, the queen of Denmark. They believed me. They believed I was one of them."

"What had you told them when they demoted Hamlet in the line of succession?"

"I told them I agreed with them. Hamlet clearly wasn't ready to become the king."

"You gave them no reason to believe you found anything wrong with the old king's assassination?"

"None whatsoever. For all anybody knew then, the old king's assassination might've hastened the day Hamlet would become the king, and I'd become the queen. Why would I wish to complain about that?"

Chapter Eight

Ophelia's Story: Ten Years before the Visit

Polonius asked Horatio to pay another visit to Prince Hamlet in Wittenberg.

When Horatio arrived at the door to Hamlet's cottage, the prince insisted he didn't want to hear the news from Elsinore Castle, no matter how serious it was or how much Horatio thought he needed to know it. He'd wait until they had their first steins in their hands.

The beer garden was crowded that spring afternoon. Hamlet made no effort to conceal his irritation at having to sit so close to his classmates, whose interpreter soon joined them. Horatio wondered if the youth worked close enough to the beer garden for the classmates to summon him whenever Hamlet showed up with a visitor from Denmark.

"I know," Hamlet said, "those assholes are talking about me again."

"They are," Horatio agreed, glad he'd begun drinking his beer.

"So out with it," Hamlet ordered. "What are they saying now?"

Horatio let the interpreter finish before he spoke himself. "They're waiting to hear the latest news from Denmark."

Hamlet gestured with his stein of beer toward the classmates and laughed. "Why do they give a fuck about the news from that stupid country? I couldn't care less myself. And I'm the prince!"

Horatio knew the classmates would run with that last remark. One after the other, they repeated it in German. "*Und ich bin der Prinz*!"

"I'll tell you why your classmates give a fuck," Horatio said, pausing to make the interpreter's job easier. "They think the news from Denmark must be very bad. They've guessed I'm afraid to tell you what it is. And they're right. I am. The news is especially bad this time."

Hamlet looked at the chortling classmates as if he'd like nothing better than being one them, sharing their merriment. Turning to Horatio again seemed to require more than a little effort.

"So tell me what it is," he said. "What's this awful news you're afraid to let me know?"

"Your father," Horatio replied, "is dead."

"*Dein Vater*," the interpreter said, "*ist tot.*"

The classmates fell silent.

Hamlet banged his stein on the table, spilling a goodly amount of his beer. "My father's dead?"

The classmates were getting what they'd come for.

"How did he die?" Hamlet asked. "He was never ill."

"Your mother and uncle say he was. Polonius says he was."

Hamlet and Horatio both saw fit to raise their steins to their lips.

"But none of your father's servants," Horatio said, "seems to have known he was ill."

"Where was he when he died?"

"In your uncle's chamber."

The classmates, maintaining their silence, hung on every word their interpreter uttered.

"What was my father doing there?"

"He was celebrating your uncle's birthday."

"Was my mother there?"

"I understand she was."

"Who else was there?"

"Polonius and Ophelia. I heard it was a small gathering."

"What was my father doing when he died?"

"He was drinking wine before dinner with the others. Then he suffered a sudden attack. He got up from his chair, vomited and fell to the floor. Polonius couldn't detect a pulse. Your father wasn't breathing."

"And his servants didn't know he'd been ill? Was he drinking my uncle's wine?"

The entire crowd in the beer garden, including the waiters, had fallen silent.

"When your father died," Horatio said, looking at the interpreter to make sure he got it right, "he was drinking your uncle's wine."

"My uncle poisoned my father," Hamlet said. "He did it to become the king."

The crowd listened intently as the interpreter passed along that information.

"What do the Danish people think?" Hamlet asked.

Horatio waited to reply to that question until the interpreter caught up with the conversation.

"The Danish people believe," Horatio said, "your uncle poisoned your father."

"That does it," Hamlet said. "I'm going to Elsinore. I'll go with you. We'll leave in the morning."

Horatio shook his head. "Your uncle and Polonius don't want you to do that. Polonius told me you should stay here. He says there's nothing you can do in Denmark. Your uncle Claudius is the king now."

"Fuck Claudius!" Hamlet yelled. "He's only the king because he murdered my father! I'm going home to set matters straight!"

As the prince and Horatio rose from their benches, the classmates and all the other beer-garden guests, including the interpreter, rose from theirs.

"*Fick Claudius*!" the crowd roared. "*Fick Claudius*!"

Ophelia's Story: Ten Years before the Visit

As soon as Hamlet returned to Elsinore Castle, he burst into the throne room unannounced.

Claudius was hearing a wine merchant's complaint against a lord and lady who were known for their boisterous—and, some would say, licentious—social gatherings. The merchant was telling the lord chamberlain and the king his side of the story. The lord and lady, he said, had neglected to reimburse him for the wine he'd delivered to them over the last year.

"Guards," Claudius yelled to the knights who were present whenever the king held court, "restrain Prince Hamlet. Search his person for weapons. Remove any you find concealed upon him. All other matters before this court are hereby adjourned until such time as I shall see fit to resume hearing them. All attendees except the members of the royal family, the lord chamberlain and the guards will withdraw and wait upon my invitation to them to return."

As the guards searched Hamlet, the other attendees filed out of the throne room buzzing about the surprise appearance of the prince.

Ophelia remained in her chair.

After the knights completed their search of Hamlet, their captain turned to Claudius. "Your Highness, the prince has no weapons upon his body."

"Keep him restrained," Claudius said.

From the moment he'd entered the throne room, Hamlet hadn't been able to take his eyes off his mother. She sat on the chair next to the king's throne, where she always sat.

"Why do you sit there?" Hamlet asked her. "That chair is the queen's chair. But you're no queen now. I've been told the king who was your husband—the king who was my father—is dead. Dead and buried. How dare you sit where you have no reason to sit?"

"I sit where I sit," Gertrude replied, "because I'm the queen."

"How can you be the queen?" Hamlet asked. "Isn't your husband dead? Isn't my father dead? Isn't he lying lost and abandoned somewhere in a dark, cold grave?"

Gertrude glared at her son. "My husband, the king, sits next to me."

Polonius looked at Hamlet with a sneer. "Yes, your father's dead. And your mother's present husband sits next to her. He's the king. I should know they're husband and wife. I presided over their marriage ceremony myself. As the lord chamberlain, I have the authority to do that. I, and only I, can marry a king and a queen—and, for that matter, a prince and a princess. I used my authority to marry the present king and your mother. It was at their request, I must say. I don't decide to do these things on my own. I have no authority to do that."

Hamlet once again made no attempt to conceal his irritation. "Shut your mouth, you old fool! I've heard enough of your babbling bullshit!"

Ophelia steeled herself against a mighty temptation to laugh.

The prince turned to his mother as he pointed his finger at Claudius. "You actually, freely, voluntarily married this piece of shit? This creature who sits where my beloved father sat? How could you do such a thing? Doesn't the thought of being married to this murdering snake make you want to vomit and shit and empty your guts from one end to the other all at once?"

Gertrude looked at her only child and chose not to reply.

"Did you observe no period of mourning for my father?" Hamlet persisted.

"Your father was gravely ill," Polonius said. "We knew he was going to die. We were in mourning for him before he died."

"He wasn't ill!" Hamlet yelled back.

He looked at Ophelia as if for assistance.

She shrugged.

"None of my father's servants knew he was ill," Hamlet continued. "To them he seemed to be a perfectly healthy person. But I know why he died oh, so suddenly. He drank poison. That's what killed him.

Somebody put poison in his wine. And the wine was his brother's wine, given to him by his brother's most loyal servant. Yes, I know why my father died! Because his brother, this cunning viper who now has the gall to place his filthy ass on the king's throne, murdered him! Murdered him with poison!"

Claudius motioned to the captain of the knights. "Remove the prince. He speaks like a madman. He's obviously lost his mind. Grief does that to people. You and the other Elsinore knights will need to keep him under surveillance in case he becomes violent."

The knights surrounded Hamlet.

Claudius turned to the lord chamberlain. "Call in the litigants. Call in the spectators as well. Court will resume."

The wine merchant trudged back into the throne room with the other persons who had claims for the king to hear. After the delay, they looked even more unhappy than they had when they'd left the throne room.

Ophelia had heard the king's knights were having difficulty enforcing his decrees. Those persons displeased with the orders were claiming he wasn't a legitimate king. His decisions, they said, therefore had even less authority behind them than the demands of an infant.

The Visit

"Hamlet didn't know his mother had married his uncle?" Fortinbras asked.

Ophelia shook her head. "Claudius and Gertrude married suddenly. Soon after Horatio left for Wittenberg."

"Wasn't Claudius much younger than Gertrude?"

"Twenty years younger."

"Do you think they were in love?"

Ophelia looked at her family in the hayfield as if she'd rather not think about the question Fortinbras had put to her. She reluctantly turned to her guest again. "I'm quite certain Claudius wasn't in love with Gertrude."

"Then why did he marry her?"

"I can only assume he didn't want her telling people he'd murdered his brother."

Fortinbras paused a moment to let that sink in. "Was Gertrude in love with Claudius?"

Ophelia hadn't imagined Fortinbras would ask such direct questions about Hamlet's mother and uncle. "More than anything else, Gertrude wished to remain the queen. I must say, though, she'd always favored Claudius. She apparently saw something in him I never did. She often remarked on what a prize he'd be for the woman fortunate enough to become his bride."

"I see," Fortinbras said.

Ophelia glanced at her family again before she continued her reply. "Claudius seemed to appreciate Gertrude's attention. I had the impression they both enjoyed playing star-crossed lovers. I often thought most people, probably including the king himself, believed that's what they were doing—play-acting. There's something else you should know about Claudius."

"What's that?"

"He only chose attractive young men for his servants."

"I see."

"And only one of them, Eric, stayed with him for more than a short period of time. Claudius sent his other servants, when he was done with them, to his friends among the lords' unmarried sons commanding the army in Norway. I understand many of those former servants died there. They'd received no training to fight in a war."

Fortinbras grimaced.

Ophelia chose to resume telling her story. "I assumed Gertrude was the reason Claudius would never admit he preferred to share his bed with other men. My aunt who owned this farm was an unmarried daughter of a lord. She had a friend, an unmarried daughter of farmers, living with her here. She died soon after my aunt came home from the castle. They weren't an unusual couple in Denmark. Two men who've never married live together on a farm a short distance down the road. They were among the first seventeen-year-olds we kept the knights from abducting and sending to Norway."

Ophelia's husband and children were bringing another load of hay back to the barn. Her younger son was leading the horse on the lane through the pasture. His brother kept reminding him, loudly, of an incident earlier that summer in which the younger son had absent-mindedly led the horse off the lane into a ditch, and the wagon had tipped over.

Ophelia took a deep breath. "Claudius once asked Horatio to become his servant. Horatio was only fifteen then, but he was tall and brawny for his age. He flatly turned Claudius down. But Claudius wasn't ready to take no for an answer. He threatened to have Horatio sent away from Elsinore Castle. Horatio would've become a vagabond. He had no relatives who could've taken him in. When Hamlet, Laertes and I found out what his uncle was doing, we complained to Hamlet's father. We later learned the king had a private talk with his brother and asked him to leave Horatio alone."

"I'm glad to hear that."

"The incident raised a question for me, though. Did the king let Claudius get away with forcing other young men to be his servants? I went to my father with the question. He rebuked me for asking it. He told me what the members of the royal family did in their private lives was none of my business."

Fortinbras scowled. "Did Gertrude know what Claudius was doing?"

"I wondered whether she did. I never came up with an answer, though."

"I can understand her wanting to remain the queen after her first husband died. But did she think she was also getting a husband in Claudius who'd do what a husband usually does?"

Ophelia sighed. "I assume Gertrude hoped for that. One of her servants told me the queen thought some men shared their beds with their male servants to keep themselves entertained when the woman they really wanted wasn't available to them. Maybe she'd deluded herself into thinking she was the unavailable woman Claudius longed for."

Ophelia's older son was now telling his brother the next time he tipped over a wagon, he'd have to right it and reload it all by himself. Nobody else in their family, not even their mother and father, would help him.

"Do you suppose," Fortinbras asked, "Gertrude knew Claudius intended to murder his brother? The king's death, after all, made her available to Claudius."

Ophelia turned to her guest with a wry smile. "That's an interesting question. I doubt, though, Gertrude had ever imagined Claudius was bold enough to attempt to assassinate his brother. She seemed as surprised by what he'd done as I was."

Chapter Nine

Ophelia's Story: Ten Years before the Visit

"I see my father in my dreams," Hamlet said.

He'd sent a servant to ask Horatio to meet him in his chamber in Elsinore Castle.

"I see him drinking from his last goblet of wine," Hamlet continued. "He pukes as much of his brother's poison out of his guts as he can. He falls to the floor. He writhes in pain. He knows he's been betrayed. He sees the darkness coming on. He feels the nothingness of death consuming him. He ceases to exist."

Hamlet took a drink from the goblet he held in his hand.

"This damned Danish beer," he said, "isn't anything like the beer we drank in Germany."

"I'm sure, though," Horatio said, "we can make do with it."

They sat at either end of Hamlet's couch.

"I've decided to kill Claudius," Hamlet said. "Isn't that what the son of a murdered king is supposed to do to the person who committed the murder?"

"You intend to kill him yourself?" Horatio asked.

"Personally," Hamlet replied. "I want to watch that fucker die an agonizing death."

Horatio shook his head. "Claudius has a platoon of knights protecting him. More than your trusting father ever had around him. You'll have to be damned careful if you want to stay alive yourself."

Hamlet took another drink of his beer. "I'll have to be clever. I'll have to take my time. I'll have to figure out how to do it without getting caught. I've got a damned good reason to want to stay alive."

"I think most people want to stay alive. But what's your damned good reason for it?"

"I'm going to marry Ophelia. She agreed to obey her father and my father and marry me."

"So I heard," Horatio said, taking another drink of his beer. "But unless you want to wait until you're the king," he said, "you'll have to get your uncle's approval to do it."

"I'm going to ask him for his approval."

"When?"

"Tomorrow."

"So soon after that uproar you caused in his court?"

"Polonius got Claudius to agree to hear my request in the king's chamber. Polonius, my mother and Ophelia will be the only other persons there."

"But don't forget, his guards will be just outside the door."

Ophelia's Story: Ten Years before the Visit

"Your Majesty," Hamlet began, "my father asked me to marry the lord chamberlain's daughter Ophelia. His purpose was to unite the royal family and the lord chamberlain's family in this dark time of war for Denmark. He said nothing could accomplish that purpose more than the marriage of the king's son and the lord chamberlain's daughter."

Claudius gave Hamlet, who stood next to Ophelia, a scornful look.

Claudius had asked the servants, less than a day after his brother had died, to remove from the king's chamber the stiff-backed wooden chair his brother had favored. The new king and Queen Gertrude sat in the stuffed chairs they'd always occupied in the king's chamber—but now placed so close together they could hold hands.

"The lord chamberlain," Hamlet continued, "has agreed to consent to my marriage to his daughter."

"And I'll only consent," Polonius said, "to the marriage of my daughter to the prince. I agree with what our late king said. Nothing can unite the royal family and mine more than the marriage of the prince and my daughter."

Claudius turned to Hamlet without hiding his disdain. "When the late king my brother spoke of your marriage to Ophelia, you were still the king's son. Now, though, you're not."

Hamlet looked as if he'd taken a blow to his gut that left him breathless.

Claudius wasn't done. "You're nothing but a loudmouth nephew who outrageously goes around telling people his uncle poisoned his father."

Hamlet blinked his eyes, this time as if he'd taken a cuff to his head.

Claudius appeared to be pleased he was causing Hamlet so much pain. "I'll *never* consent to your marriage to the lord chamberlain's daughter."

Polonius reeled from that promise no less than Hamlet. "Your Majesty," the lord chamberlain said, "Prince Hamlet may no longer be the king's son, but he does occupy the first position in the line of succession to Denmark's throne. He needs a wife who'll be his and the people's queen when the time comes. Who could better be that queen than my beautiful and intelligent daughter? I'm told the people love her as much as Hamlet does."

Claudius looked at Polonius and shook his head. "I'm certain the time when this insolent youth succeeds to Denmark's throne will be many, many years in the future, assuming he lives that long. In any event, it's nothing I need worry about now."

"Perhaps," Polonius said, "Prince Hamlet can offer his most sincere apology to you and to Her Majesty the queen for the hateful, thoughtless and utterly false remarks he made in court."

Claudius looked at his lord chamberlain through narrowed eyes.

"The young prince," Polonius said, "had recently learned of his father's death. I understand he didn't know his father had been gravely ill. It was my fault he remained unaware of the situation. I should've thought to send a servant to Germany to inform him. I'm certain the shock of the news of his father's sudden death led to his unfortunate appearance in your court and the uncalled-for words he spoke. Please let him apologize to you so he can live in hope someday his wife will be, as he so dearly hopes, my kind, caring and thoughtful daughter."

Claudius shook his head again. "It'll take more than an apology before I'll consent to a marriage between this obnoxious nephew of mine and your daughter."

"Can you inform us, Your Highness," Polonius asked, "what it will take for the prince to obtain your consent to marry my daughter?"

Claudius sneered. "For one thing, he has to prove his loyalty to me. He has to show me and every other person in Denmark he fully supports my leadership of this land."

"I'm sure, Your Majesty," Polonius said, "the prince will wish to do everything he can to demonstrate he supports you in every way possible. Need I remind you, Your Highness, he's in love with my daughter? I'm sure he'll do anything you ask him to do to obtain her as his bride."

Claudius looked at Hamlet from head to toe as if he were sizing him up for a position as his servant. "I have in mind a specific task this prince can undertake to prove his loyalty to me. He can lead our forces when I give them the order to invade our perfidious northern neighbor."

Polonius gasped. "Your Majesty, Prince Hamlet has had no military training."

Claudius turned to Hamlet. "Then this lazy, beer-guzzling, unqualified prince can get off his dead ass. He can dedicate himself to training with the court's most experienced knights. I'll order them to provide him with the most rigorous course of military instruction they can devise. I'll let them know this recruit will lead them into our territories now under the sway of the Norwegian king. This prince will restore those territories to our rule. And he'll bring back to me that other prince, that swaggering Fortinbras, for a celebratory, public beheading. After he's accomplished all those things, then, and only then, will I consider whether to consent to his marriage to the lord chamberlain's daughter."

"That's something I'd love to see," Queen Gertrude said. "The prince I gave birth to leading our army in a great victory against our enemy. If he did that, even I might welcome his marriage to the lord chamberlain's daughter."

"You can leave now, Prince Hamlet," Claudius said. "The queen and I are done with you. And remember, you can be damned grateful I haven't chosen to charge you with treason. Try not to shoot off your mouth again. Otherwise, you'll feel the executioner's blade slicing through your neck. And it won't do your mother any good to beg me not to order you to the chopping block. I'll do it anyway."

The Visit

"You remained silent," Fortinbras said.

"I chose not to waste my breath," Ophelia said. "None of the other persons cared what I thought or wanted. I was a prize Prince Hamlet could win if he came to terms with Claudius."

"What was Hamlet thinking? He could accuse Claudius of killing his father one day, and a few days later he could obtain his consent to marry you for the asking?"

"Hamlet was born a prince. He didn't grow up in the real world of give and take. He simply took whatever he wanted. He could get away with it when he was a child. The three friends he wandered about the castle and castle grounds with taught him not to be nasty to the servants. As a result, most of them found him charming and gave him whatever he wanted. He didn't become a mean and foolish prince like Claudius. He became a mere fool instead."

"Did Claudius imagine his nephew could ever actually lead an invasion of Norway?"

Ophelia scoffed. "Claudius knew that would never happen. He also knew an invasion, whoever led it, would never happen. The army commanders who could speak freely with him had told him an invasion wasn't possible. I'm sure, though, Claudius wanted Hamlet to train with the knights. He knew war-loving Gertrude would go along with that. He no doubt figured at some point he could entice a knight or two into killing Hamlet. It probably would've taken only enough money to pay off their gambling debts."

"That makes sense, but I'm not sure I understand your father. He went along with the demotion of Prince Hamlet in the line of succession, but he was still insisting on your marriage to him."

"My father had two goals then. First, he wanted his only son, Laertes, to succeed him as the lord chamberlain. That's why he went along with Hamlet's demotion. It had brought Laertes and Claudius together as allies. My father was very much in favor of that."

"What was your father's second goal."

"He also wanted me, his only daughter, to marry a prince, any prince. After Hamlet's demotion, my father told Claudius I'd be the perfect wife for him. When Gertrude heard about that, she was furious. I think it was the main reason she insisted on her marriage to Claudius within a few days of the old king's death. Then my father had to go back to his original position. He'd only consent to my marriage to Hamlet. Every other man in the world, he told me, was out of the running."

Ophelia looked toward the lane in the pasture. Her husband and children were on their way to the hayfield again. Her husband, sitting at the front of the wagon, held the horse's reins in his hands now. Their children, in their loose summer clothes, lay flat on their backs behind him like rag dolls.

"My father told me," Ophelia said, "I should prepare for a lifetime as Hamlet's wife, whether I had any affection for him or not. He hoped Hamlet and I would have a dozen children. It was my duty to give birth to as many as I could. My father said they'd ensure his line would go on forever. In the history books, he'd be known as the wise ancestor of numerous kings and queens. I guess I'd be known, if I were known at all, as the great man's dutiful, heir-producing daughter."

Fortinbras gestured toward the hay wagon. "You have four heirs out there."

"But without a drop of royal blood in their veins. That's no prince on the wagon with them."

Fortinbras turned to Ophelia. "There's something I've noticed in your story. It concerns your father and brother and the members of the royal family."

"What's that?"

"They seem to have done what they did without any regard to how it appeared to the people."

Ophelia nodded. "They truly didn't give a damn what the people thought of them. I knew that as soon as I knew anything in my life. And that's what took them down."

Chapter Ten

Ophelia's Story: Ten Years before the Visit

Hamlet looked at Horatio, who was once again sitting at the other end of his couch. "My uncle has asked me to go to Norway."

They were drinking beer from the steins the prince had brought back from Wittenberg.

Horatio took a swig. "To Norway?"

"Norway. Claudius wants me to deliver a peace offer to Prince Fortinbras."

"A peace offer? I thought your uncle wanted to invade Norway. Any peace agreement now would guarantee Denmark started and fought a nine-year-old war for absolutely nothing."

"Claudius says his peace offer will make the war a success for Denmark."

"If it does that, why would Fortinbras agree to it? Do you have the peace offer?"

Hamlet nodded. "I have it."

"Can I read what it says?"

"It's under seal, the king's seal. Only Fortinbras can break the seal."

Horatio set his stein of beer down on the low table in front of them. "Did you agree to take the peace offer to Norway?"

"I did."

"Why in hell did you do that?"

"My uncle said he'll reward me if I'm successful."

"How's he going to reward you?"

"He'll consent to my marriage to Ophelia."

Horatio took another swig of his beer. "How do you intend to get to Norway?"

"I'll take a coach to a port. I'll book passage on a neutral country's ship to cross the sea. I have diplomatic papers from Polonius that'll get me off the ship and into Norway."

Horatio shook his head. "Aren't you afraid your uncle is setting you up?"

"Setting me up for what?"

"For your murder."

"My murder?"

"Your murder."

"I have no doubt my uncle would love to see me dead. He wouldn't have me around anymore accusing him of killing my father. But how's he going to murder me?"

"Couldn't he have his knights accost you somewhere between here and Norway? They could kill you and make it look as if highwaymen did it."

Hamlet scoffed. "I'm the prince. I'm first in the line of succession to the throne. My uncle can't order his knights to kill me without a trial."

"Maybe he can't, legally. But does that mean he won't? He couldn't legally kill your father, but he did it anyway. And who'd decide his innocence or guilt if he were put on trial for it? He would."

Hamlet lifted his stein to his lips as if he were stranded on a desert island dying of thirst.

Horatio took a deep breath. "I think I'd better go with you to Norway. I'll see the Swedish ambassador."

"Is she the one," Hamlet asked, "who lets you use her library?"

Horatio nodded. "Maybe she can get us to Norway and back alive."

Ophelia's Story: Ten Years before the Visit

Horatio once again entered the rear door to the Swedish ambassador's house before dawn. His companion this time was Hamlet.

A servant escorted them to the library.

Hamlet peered at the books on the shelves lining the walls. "I can see they've got one section of books in Danish. What are the others?"

"They've got nine sections," Horatio replied. "One each for books in Swedish, Danish, Norwegian, English, French, German, Dutch and Latin. And another for everything else—Icelandic, Finnish, Polish, Russian, Spanish, Italian, Greek, Turkish, even some in Arabic. I haven't learned to read the languages in that section yet."

"But you will?"

"Maybe, if I live long enough."

When Christina entered the room, Horatio introduced her to Hamlet.

"My carriage is ready," she said. "If our journey results in peace between Denmark and Norway, my aunt will be ecstatic. She tells me the pause in the war lately has made her as happy as she's been in the last nine years."

Ophelia's Story: Ten Years before the Visit

Horatio and Christina were both careful not to let Hamlet know they'd previously ridden together in her carriage on a journey that took her passengers to Norway.

When they reached the Danish army's encampment, Christina peered through the windows on both sides of the carriage and sighed. "This isn't much of an army anymore. I understand the knights no longer make any effort to train. Look at them. I've heard they spend their days gambling, drinking and whoring."

Horatio could see they were letting their garbage pile up. Many of their tents looked as if a windstorm of any strength could flatten them. He was certain the vagabonds he'd come upon camping in the forest near the farm would be ashamed to call this disorderly bivouac their home.

"I'm told," Christina said, "many of the knights won't consider taking part in any invasion of Norway."

"Can I guess," Horatio asked, "the reason they give for that?"

"Please do," Christina said.

"They'll only fight for a legitimate king," Horatio said.

Christina gave him a wink. "I'd say that's a good guess."

Ophelia's Story: Ten Years before the Visit

"Do you remember," Fortinbras asked Hamlet, "the time my father and I came to see you and your family at Elsinore Castle? I was thirteen years old then. I believe you were six."

Hamlet nodded. "I remember. My mother told me you'd be my lifelong rival."

Fortinbras didn't seem surprised. "My father begged your father and his lord chamberlain not to invade Norway. Sadly, for too many people, his begging didn't accomplish a thing."

Horatio nodded. "Sadly, indeed."

They sat at the same table Fortinbras and Horatio had shared with Ophelia. Neither Fortinbras nor Horatio, though, made any mention of their previous meeting.

Fortinbras turned to Hamlet. "I've been told you have a message for me from Claudius."

Hamlet laid his uncle's sealed message on the table.

Fortinbras broke the seal and opened the envelope. He removed the message and glanced at it.

He looked at Hamlet. "I can't possibly do what your uncle wants me to do."

"What does he want you to do?" Hamlet asked.

Fortinbras frowned. "He wants me to kill you."

Ophelia's Story: Ten Years before the War

Fortinbras held up the peace offer so that Hamlet and Horatio could see it was a blank piece of paper.

Fortinbras laid the paper on the table and looked at Hamlet. "I met with a person yesterday who claimed to be your uncle's real messenger. He said your presenting me with a blank piece of paper under your uncle's seal would prove he was who he said he was."

"Did he bring you a peace offer?" Horatio asked.

"Oh, yes," Fortinbras replied. "It was an oral peace offer."

Horatio rolled his eyes. "So Claudius could deny he ever made it."

Fortinbras nodded. "I assumed that was the purpose of an oral offer. It was actually a rhymed couplet. The messenger told me the rhyme made it easier for him to remember. 'Hamlet's death will gain you more,' the messenger recited, 'than an end to the war.'"

Looking as if he'd been slapped, Hamlet remained silent.

"Claudius seems to promise to end the war," Horatio said to Fortinbras, "if you murder Hamlet. I take it the *more* he speaks of is your elevation from the second to the first position in the line of succession to Denmark's throne."

Fortinbras nodded. "That's how I interpreted the message."

"But even if you were willing to murder Hamlet," Horatio said, "there's no way you could hold Claudius to his promise to end the war. You could kill Hamlet today, and Claudius could launch an invasion of Norway tomorrow."

Fortinbras nodded again. "That's true. I'd also have no guarantee I'd remain in the first position in the line of succession to Denmark's throne.

Claudius engineered Hamlet's demotion. Why couldn't he simply decree mine? We have a number of cousins in Sweden and Germany he could promote above me."

"You're right not to trust Claudius," Horatio said. "Did the person you met with yesterday claim to be his servant?"

"He did," Fortinbras replied. "He told me he's served Claudius since they were boys."

"Did he say his name was Eric?" Horatio asked.

Fortinbras nodded. "He did."

"He was the fucker," Hamlet said, "who served my father a goblet of poisoned wine."

Fortinbras looked at Hamlet. "Why did you agree to bring me a peace offer from your uncle? Were you hoping to end the war?"

Hamlet scoffed. "I don't give a damn whether the war ends or not."

Fortinbras stared at Hamlet. "I've heard the Danish people want the war to end."

Hamlet shrugged. "I don't know what the Danish people want."

Horatio shook his head. "The war can't end soon enough for the Danish people."

"That's what Ophelia says," Hamlet said. "You and she might be right about that, but you also might be wrong."

"Ophelia?" Fortinbras asked. "Who's Ophelia?"

"The lord chamberlain's daughter," Horatio replied.

"The woman I love," Hamlet said. "My uncle Claudius and I had an agreement. I'd bring that phony damned peace offer to you, and he'd consent to my marriage to Ophelia. He was obviously lying to me. My friend here thought the cocksucker was up to no good. And he tried to tell me that, but I wouldn't listen. I'm the prince. I've always been the prince. I can't remember not being the prince. If somebody tells me something I don't want to hear, I don't pay any attention to it."

Fortinbras studied Hamlet's contorted face like an archaeologist marveling at an artifact buried and forgotten thousands of years ago.

"Does Ophelia wish to marry you?" Fortinbras asked.

"I'm in love with her," Hamlet replied. "I'm the prince."

"Ophelia's father," Horatio said, "doesn't give her any choice in the matter. He wants her to marry the prince. He won't consent to her marriage to anybody else."

"Ophelia's in love with me," Hamlet said. "She won't say she is.

She's always been contrary that way. You say one thing, and you can damned well bet she'll say the opposite. But I know she loves me as much as I love her."

Horatio turned to Fortinbras with a sardonic smile. He otherwise chose not to agree or disagree with Hamlet's remarks.

"But now I also know," Hamlet said, "my uncle will never consent to my marriage to her. He'll withhold his approval just to vex me. He hates me as much as I hate him. I'll have to kill him someway, secretly. When I'm the king, I'll order Ophelia to obey her father and marry me."

"Whether she wants to or not?" Fortinbras asked.

"I'll order her to do the right thing, for herself, for myself, for her father, and for Denmark."

"And when you're the king," Fortinbras asked, "what about the war? Will you end it?"

Hamlet shook his head. "I don't know how I could do that. The lords have lost too many of their knights in the war. Most of them have lost sons in it, too. They've spent a lot of treasure on it. They'd think any king who stopped the war was stabbing them in the back. A king who did that might not live past the day he did it. The Danish people have already seen how easy it is to get rid of one. You simply tell your most loyal servant to give him a goblet of poisoned wine."

The Visit

"I was hoping," Fortinbras said, "Hamlet and I could've reached an agreement to end the war. If, of course, he became the king of Denmark."

"Couldn't you have offered him some help in that regard?" Ophelia asked. "I mean, to assassinate Claudius?"

Fortinbras nodded. "Christina might've been able to sneak some well-paid assassins into Denmark. I believe they usually employ Russians for that sort of thing. The assassins would've needed assistance from somebody in Elsinore Castle, though, to do their work and escape with their lives."

Ophelia's husband and children had returned to the hayfield and were loading the wagon again.

Ophelia turned to her guest. "Did you consider I might've provided that assistance?"

Fortinbras nodded again. "You were very much on my mind then. I assumed your help would've been highly valuable to anybody bent on killing Claudius."

"But Horatio told me you never discussed killing Claudius with Hamlet."

"I didn't."

"Can I ask you why you didn't?"

"I didn't think killing Claudius at that time would've been what you wanted. After Hamlet became the king of Denmark, he and your father would've forced you into a marriage with him. I didn't think that would've done anybody any good. And Hamlet wasn't interested in ending the war anyway."

Chapter Eleven

Ophelia's Story: Ten Years before the Visit

The morning after Hamlet returned from Norway, he stomped into the throne room while Claudius was holding court. The prince had asked Horatio to come with him.

"We'll take a brief recess," Claudius said to the litigants in the proceeding he was hearing.

Ophelia could see the king had been struggling to remain awake. His eyes drooped like lines of newly washed clothes on a still, humid day.

As the spectators, disputants and witnesses made way, Hamlet, with Horatio close behind him, approached his uncle. "Your Majesty, are you surprised to see me home from Norway?"

Claudius narrowed his eyes but otherwise refused to respond to Hamlet's query.

But the question roused the queen from her own stupor. "Why, my son, should His Majesty be surprised to see you?"

Hamlet scoffed. "Many of our people who've been sent to Norway in the last nine years have lost their lives there. No, they haven't come home. And unless they walk the earth now as ghosts, they'll never come home. Being or not being is no longer a choice for them."

Claudius made no attempt to conceal his displeasure with his nephew's cheek. "Did you speak with your haughty northern cousin, Prince Fortinbras?"

"I most certainly did."

"Did you give him my peace offer?"

The throne-room crowd, who'd heard nothing of a peace offer from King Claudius to Prince Fortinbras, murmured.

"I did indeed give Fortinbras your peace offer," Hamlet replied.

"Did he read it?" Claudius asked.

"Horatio and I watched him read it. I'm sorry to report, though, he dismissed Your Majesty's peace offer out of hand."

Claudius glowered at Hamlet. "Did you read my peace offer?"

Hamlet snickered. "Of course not. Your peace offer was under seal. It was meant, I assumed, for the eyes of Prince Fortinbras only."

"So now we see," Claudius said, "my Norwegian nephew for the arrogant upstart he is—summarily dismissing such a generous and thoughtful peace offer."

"May the bastard die tomorrow!" Queen Gertrude cried.

Hamlet ignored his mother and turned to the king. "Could you tell us, Your Majesty, what your generous and thoughtful peace offer consisted of?"

"I offered," Claudius replied, "to split the disputed territories down the middle, half of them to Norway, and the other half to Denmark."

The spectators openly groaned. The offer would've required Norway to give up half the land it had spent nine horrific years successfully defending.

Hamlet laughed. "Prince Fortinbras was quite specific as to what he thought you should do with your peace offer."

The king, who seemed to shrink on his throne like a failed loaf of bread, remained silent.

Polonius, though, standing next to Claudius, couldn't resist taking Hamlet's bait. "What did the Norwegian prince say His Majesty should do with his generous and thoughtful peace offer?"

Hamlet turned to Claudius. "He said Your Majesty should shove it up the most receptive orifice this world has ever known—your asshole."

Initially, the spectators were too stunned to respond.

Claudius, though, rose to his feet, his face crimson with rage.

"This court," he bellowed, "is adjourned!"

But before he and Queen Gertrude reached the doorway through which they entered and exited the throne room, the crowd had given itself up to howls of laughter.

The Visit

"I wasn't laughing," Ophelia said. "Hamlet should've been figuring out, for his own sake, how to get rid of Claudius. For the sake of Denmark, he should've been trying to find a way to end the war. Instead, he chose to waste his time pointlessly insulting Claudius. The crowd loved his performance. But he only convinced me, if I'd needed any more convincing by then, he was, at best, a buffoon."

"I gather," Fortinbras said, "Hamlet could've used the crowd in his struggle against Claudius."

"He could've and should've done that. The people were almost unanimously on his side. Claudius had murdered his father and stolen his inheritance."

Ophelia's Story: Ten Years before the Visit

Hamlet sent a servant to ask Ophelia if he could speak with her in her chamber.

"Only if he isn't drunk," Ophelia told the servant, "and has nothing to drink with him. Please also tell him I won't offer him any of my wine, to say nothing of my schnapps."

When Hamlet appeared at her door, she could smell alcohol on his breath, but she agreed he didn't appear to be intoxicated. She asked him to sit on her couch. She sat on one of the chairs facing him.

"My loving uncle," he began, with the usual whine in his voice, this time leavened with sarcasm, "asked the Norwegian prince to kill me. That was his fucking peace offer. If the prince killed me, Claudius would've ended the war."

"And Fortinbras," Ophelia asked, "compassionately refused to accept your uncle's offer?"

Hamlet shrugged. "I don't know if compassion had anything to do with it. Fortinbras said he had no way to hold Claudius to his promise to end the war after I was dead."

"How very insightful. But didn't Fortinbras consider he'd become second in the line of succession after he killed you?"

"It was part of my uncle's offer. But Fortinbras saw through that as well. If my father could demote me, his son, in the line of succession, why couldn't Claudius demote an enemy prince?"

"Another point well taken. Maybe we should invite a prince that perceptive to be the king of Denmark."

Hamlet scowled. "Not until I'm dead, I hope."

"Of course. That's what I meant."

"Anyway, I'm afraid of my uncle."

"You should be."

"I can't leave the castle unless I'm with Horatio."

"We both know he's always a good person to have at your side. But he can't be the answer to your problem. You've got to kill your uncle before he kills you."

"I have another reason to kill him."

"What's that?"

"He'll never consent to my marriage to you."

"Even if you had his consent, I wouldn't marry a prince who might very well be dead the day after our wedding night."

"You mean, you'll only marry me if I'm the king of Denmark?"

"That's right. So do you have a plan to make it happen?"

"A plan?"

"A plan to murder your uncle and get away with it. That's possible in Denmark. Your uncle murdered your father and got away with it. He sits on the throne now, and nobody bothers to ask if he's the legitimate king."

Hamlet blinked his eyes. "I'll have to wait until I get a good opportunity to kill him."

Ophelia scoffed. "That might take us into our old age. Your uncle has more than a few knights assigned to do nothing more than protect him."

"I'll have to do something."

"You're damned right you will. And if you don't have a plan, I do.

"You have a plan for me to kill Claudius?"

"And get away with it. My father told me your mother has agreed to speak with you privately in her chamber."

"That's right. I'll meet with her this evening. She imposed the same condition you did. I have to be sober."

"My father can't tell you this himself, but he doesn't think you should meet with your mother in her chamber."

"Why not?"

"Your uncle plans to be present in her chamber when you're there."

"My mother promised me only she and I would be present."

"Yes, she did. But she also told Claudius about your meeting. As a result, he plans to be there when you are. He'll be hiding behind her draperies. He told my father he wants to eavesdrop on you and your mother. He wants to know if you and she are plotting against him."

"That's silly. My mother would never plot against him. He's always been her favorite."

"Of course it's silly. That's why my father doesn't believe Claudius."

Hamlet knitted his brow. "I don't understand."

"My father thinks Claudius plans to murder you in your mother's chamber. So do I."

"You think he plans to murder me? Then I'd better not go there. I'll have to meet my mother somewhere else."

Ophelia, losing her patience, glared at Hamlet. "Don't you see? This is your chance to kill Claudius. Have your dagger hidden in your clothes. The knights outside your mother's door won't search you. You're the prince. Claudius will be alone behind your mother's curtains. He won't have any knights with him to protect him there. And it shouldn't be difficult for you to detect where he is. Watch for the slightest movement of the curtains. When you see where he is, stab him through them with your dagger. Keep stabbing him until you're certain he's dead. When you call the knights in to take away his body, tell them he was an intruder behind the curtains. You didn't know the intruder was Claudius. Your mother will have to go along with you. The moment Claudius dies, you'll be the king. Nobody will dare question what you've done. Anybody who tries to raise the slightest doubt will be guilty of treason."

Hamlet stared at Ophelia. "You want me to kill Claudius this evening?"

"The sooner the better."

"In my mother's chamber?"

"You'll be alone with your mother and Claudius. You'll never have a better chance to kill him. He won't have his knights or anybody else to protect him. You'll claim you killed an unknown intruder through your mother's curtains. Who can say you didn't? Be sure to show the bloody, tattered curtains to the knights who come running in. They're no fools. They'll realize you're the king as soon as they see Claudius is dead. They'll do whatever you tell them to do."

"You want me to kill Claudius just like that?"

"Just like that."

"He'll be dead. I'll be the king."

"He'll be dead. You'll be the king."

"I've never killed a person. I've never stabbed a person. I've never even stabbed an animal. I've never killed anything bigger than a fly."

"Remember what you'll be doing—taking revenge for what Claudius did to your innocent father."

Hamlet shrugged. "You know, I can't really blame Claudius for killing that pompous old fool. He sat so rigid in those stiff-backed chairs he liked. He never seemed like a father to me. Nor did my mother seem like a mother. The servants were my parents. They were like a flock of loving sheep, and I was their lamb. You remember. You and I and Horatio and Laertes were all their lambs."

Ophelia once again found herself staring at Hamlet in disbelief. "You need to concentrate on killing Claudius. If you don't, he'll kill you. He's already killed a king. What's a prince compared to a king?"

"You want me to stab him to death with my dagger? You want me to be his executioner?"

"Who better to do it? You're the prince. You'll become the king the moment he dies."

"His blood will be everywhere."

"The servants will gladly clean it up. They're my friends. I'll get down on my hands and knees with them and help. We'll sing songs while we work. Happy songs. Songs people sing at victory celebrations after successful wars—and assassinations."

"And then we'll have our own wedding?"

"If that's what you want."

"Is that what you want?"

"It makes no difference what I want if that's what you and my father want. You'll be the king, and he'll still be the lord chamberlain. What I want will be irrelevant."

Hamlet viewed Ophelia warily. "Are you certain there's no other man you'd rather marry than me?"

"There's no such man. After you and my father made it clear to me I had no choice but you, I stopped looking for another man to marry. I only need one man for that. Now focus on killing Claudius this evening. You and the people of Denmark need to see him dead—tonight."

Chapter Twelve

Ophelia's Story: Ten Years before the Visit

In the earliest years of her childhood, Ophelia had become familiar with the queen's chamber. She and the prince discovered back doors so remote from the main corridors in Elsinore Castle the servants left them unlocked. During subsequent explorations of the chamber, Ophelia and Hamlet found hiding places behind the many ceiling-to-floor draperies Gertrude was fond of. When the queen summoned the misbehaving prince to her chamber for a scolding—sometimes even for a spanking with the back of her hairbrush on his bare buttocks—Ophelia would secretly observe, doing her best not to laugh and give herself away.

When nineteen-year-old Hamlet showed up for his private conversation with his mother, Ophelia was in her favorite hiding place. She could pull the overlapping curtains apart a slight distance and see as well as hear whatever happened in Gertrude's parlor.

The prince barged into the room and sat down on his mother's couch without receiving an invitation to do so. "You married that hideous man who murdered my father. You took yourself to the assassin's bed, as his lawful wife, within hours of your first husband's funeral. Have you no shame at all?"

Ophelia sighed. She couldn't understand why Hamlet had chosen to berate his mother and insult his uncle. She and he had agreed his sole purpose in his mother's parlor was to kill Claudius before Claudius killed him.

"Your father wasn't murdered," Queen Gertrude said. "He died after a long illness."

Hamlet scoffed. "An illness only you, your lover Claudius and that lackey lord chamberlain knew anything about. My father's own servants had no knowledge of the strange malady you claim killed him. They told me that themselves."

Gertrude sat stiffly in a stuffed chair Claudius had brought back from Italy for her. Upon her receipt of it, she declared it her special chair and ordered her servants not to allow any other person to sit in it—ever.

"No," Hamlet said, "my father died from the poison mixed in the wine my treacherous uncle gave him to drink."

The queen shook her head. "A servant gave your father that goblet of wine."

"My uncle's most loyal servant gave my father that goblet of wine. Why do you suppose he did it? On his own whim? Or because Claudius had ordered him to do it?"

Ophelia began to wonder if Hamlet would ever summon the nerve to kill Claudius. He should've been examining the wall curtains to discover where his uncle was hiding. He had no need to discuss with his mother anything more consequential than the weather. Instead, he was senselessly treating her as if she were on trial for her life and he were her mad-dog prosecutor.

"If you'd grown up to be the prince you could've become," Queen Gertrude said, "Denmark wouldn't be facing its utter defeat at the hands of your far more talented, brave and resourceful Norwegian cousin."

Hamlet appeared too taken aback by that remark to make an immediate response.

"Prince Fortinbras," Gertrude said, "knows what it means to be a true prince. Too bad your aunt didn't live to see what he's done."

"What in hell are you telling me?" Hamlet asked. "I'm already a failure as a prince?"

"If you'd gone to Norway as soon as you were old enough to go, you could've learned how to lead our army. You could've forced your father to appoint you the army's supreme commander. You could've turned your father's looming defeat into a magnificent victory. You could've returned every smidgen of the disputed territories to Denmark. You could've outshone that Norwegian prince on the field of battle. You could've killed him and stolen his glory."

Once again, Hamlet remained silent.

Gertrude had more. "You've could've returned to Elsinore Castle a hero. The people would've covered you and your horse with a blanket of flowers. You would've been the valiant prince a great queen deserves to stand next to on a balcony above an admiring, cheering crowd."

Hamlet shook his head. "You know what would've happened to me if I'd gone to Norway? I would've been killed. With my luck, I sure as shit would've been killed."

"At least you would've died a hero."

Hamlet gasped.

But his mother still wasn't done. "You could've been a living hero if you'd ever learned to fight in a war. All the eligible princesses in the world would've thrown themselves at your feet. You could've taken your pick of them. You surely would've thumbed your nose at that servant-loving slut you cling to like an ill-bred, flea-infested dog."

"Slut? Who are you calling a slut?"

Gertrude laughed. "The lord chamberlain's daughter, that's who."

The labored breathing of a person apparently suffering a seizure came from behind the drapes on the opposite side of the room from Ophelia's hiding place.

Hamlet rose from his mother's couch, removed his dagger from its sheath and approached the source of the noise.

"An intruder!" he yelled.

As Ophelia had asked him to do, he stabbed the intruder through the curtains repeatedly.

When the curtains became soaked with blood from the point of the stabbings to the floor, Hamlet pulled them down from the rod holding them at the ceiling.

Looking at the blood-covered body crumpled at his feet, Hamlet could see he hadn't killed his uncle Claudius. He'd stabbed to death the lord chamberlain, Polonius.

Ophelia's Story: Ten Years before the Visit

"Guards, guards, come quickly!" Queen Gertrude screamed to the knights outside the front door to her chamber. "Hamlet has killed an intruder! He's saved my life!"

With the attention of the queen, the prince and the guards focused on her dead father, Ophelia slipped out of her hiding place, left the queen's chamber and hurried to her own.

Ophelia's Story: Ten Years before the Visit

When Ophelia heard the loud and rapid knocking on her door, she knew her visitor would be Hamlet. Opening the door, she wasn't surprised to see him still clutching his dagger and wearing clothes soaked with blood.

"I killed your father," Hamlet said, trembling as he entered her chamber.

Ophelia closed the door behind him. "You killed my father? What are you talking about?"

Hamlet looked at his dagger as if it were alive, a demon. "Your father was behind the curtains. Claudius wasn't the intruder. Your father was."

"You killed my father? This is his blood?"

"I killed your father. I stabbed him. I stabbed him until I was certain he was dead. This is his blood."

Ophelia curled her lip. "My father and Claudius must've changed their plans. My father must've agreed to do the eavesdropping. Maybe he did it to keep Claudius from attempting to kill you."

Hamlet held up his blood-soaked dagger. "I used this to kill your father."

"Put it away," Ophelia said. "I don't need to see that."

Hamlet slid his dagger into its sheath. "What do we do now?"

"There's nothing we need to do now."

"But I just killed your father."

"He was an intruder in the queen's chamber. He was there to eavesdrop on a private conversation between the queen and the prince. He was taking his chances he'd be discovered. Why do you and I need to do anything? I'm certain his kindly servants will see to his funeral and burial. If they need any assistance from me, they know I'll be here, in mourning, as any proper lord chamberlain's daughter would be."

"Your father was in favor of our marriage."

"Yes, he was, very much so."

"I didn't mean to kill him."

"Nobody will ever imagine you did. The intruder in your mother's chamber could've been anybody. The people will consider you a hero for possibly saving her life."

"I'm not a hero. I didn't kill your father, of all people, to save my mother's life."

"I'm saying you did. You'd better start saying the same thing."

Hamlet looked at Ophelia, blinking.

She reopened the door to her chamber. "I think you should go to your chamber now and ask your servants for some hot bath water. They can wash the blood out of your clothes tomorrow. Don't insist they do it tonight. You know how to be nice to your servants."

The Lord Chamberlain's Daughter

Ophelia's Story: Ten Years before the Visit

"Claudius asked me to come here," Horatio said.

He sat with Laertes in his garret.

Ophelia had heard the lords' sons no longer wished to visit Laertes. He was too weighed down with fear, they said. If Hamlet and Ophelia became the king and queen, he was certain he'd have to flee Denmark and live incognito in another country. Otherwise, they'd hunt him down and have him murdered for opposing their marriage. The lords' sons wished to spend their days and nights in the bistros Paris was famous for, even in Denmark, but Laertes had no interest in that sort of thing.

"I have some awful news for you," Horatio said.

He and Laertes once again drank claret as they viewed the Seine.

"What other kind of news could I expect," Laertes asked, "if it comes from Denmark? Wouldn't you agree it's the most hopeless country in the world?"

"No, I wouldn't agree with that. Denmark has been very good to me. And I'm an orphan. In any event, Claudius sent me here to tell you you're an orphan now yourself."

"I'm an orphan?"

"Hamlet killed your father."

Laertes set his goblet down on the low table in front of them. "Did I hear you correctly? Did you say *Hamlet* killed my father?"

"I did say that. I saw your father lying in state in Elsinore Castle myself. I spoke with Hamlet. He readily admits he stabbed your father to death."

"He admits he murdered my father? He admits he murdered the lord chamberlain?"

"He doesn't admit he murdered your father. He says he was engaged in a conversation with his mother in her chamber. He discovered an intruder behind a curtain. He stabbed the intruder, repeatedly, through the curtain. Then he learned the intruder was your father. He claims your father must've been eavesdropping on him and the queen. And he was certain your father was doing it, he told me, because Claudius had ordered him to do it."

"What does Queen Gertrude say?"

"She says Hamlet is telling the truth. He killed an intruder behind a curtain. Only later did they discover the intruder was your father."

"She'd protect her darling boy no matter what he did. What does my sister say?"

"She wasn't present, but she says she has no reason not to believe Hamlet and Gertrude."

Laertes wrinkled his brow. "Hamlet murders our father in cold blood, and Ophelia sees nothing wrong with it. That just goes to show how desperate she is to marry Hamlet and become the queen. Then they'll make me the lowest of the low."

"I don't think Ophelia and Hamlet mean to harm you."

"You don't know them as well as I do. Anyway, what does King Claudius say about this murder of his lord chamberlain?"

"He agrees with you. He thinks Hamlet murdered your father. Claudius even thinks he knows why. He believes your father told Hamlet and his mother he'd changed his mind about Ophelia's marriage to Hamlet. He'd come to realize Hamlet was an addle-brained prince. He'd no longer consent to his daughter's marriage to such a person. Rather than accepting your father's decision, Hamlet became angry with him. When your father refused to consider changing his mind again, Hamlet, in a rage, stabbed your father with his dagger—and kept stabbing him until he was certain he was dead."

"That's exactly what must've happened. Hamlet murdered my father because he'd changed his mind about Ophelia. I'm damned glad I helped convince the lords to put Claudius first in the line of succession, ahead of Hamlet. I'm also damned glad Claudius is the king now. I shudder to think about the possibility of Hamlet in that position. He'd simply murder anybody who disagreed with him. I could see that when we were boys. I always imagined he'd become a tyrant king. He never let me speak my mind. You remember that. He was always telling me to shut my cock-sucking mouth. And all the silly business about Ophelia being his wife and queen. Hamlet took it seriously, as if something so awful and disgusting was really going to happen. And now he's murdered my father. Denmark is as rotten as a country can get. I can smell its stench, even here—and they call this city the perfume capital of the world."

Ophelia's Story: Ten Years before the Visit

Horatio raised his goblet to his lips, set it down again on the low table and turned to Laertes. "I also have some good news for you."

Laertes scoffed. "What possible good news could you have for me now? Hamlet has murdered my father. I must be the very next person on that madman's list."

"Claudius asked me to tell you he wants you to be his new lord chamberlain."

In an instant, Laertes's mood changed from the darkness of a stormy midnight to the brightness of a sunny noon. "That *is* good news," he said, grinning, "the best damned news I've heard in a long time. I'll return to Denmark with you. We'll leave at dawn tomorrow. I've got people to settle scores with. I've got a prince to pay back for viciously murdering my father."

The Visit

"I assume," Fortinbras said, "Horatio knew you were present when Hamlet stabbed your father."

"Horatio knew that," Ophelia said.

"But he told Laertes you weren't there."

"We didn't think it would be helpful if Laertes or anybody else knew I was present when Hamlet killed my father. I told you we'd taught ourselves how to lie. It took a lot of practice, a lot of effort, to do it right—and get away with it."

Chapter Thirteen

Ophelia's Story: Ten Years before the Visit

King Claudius and Queen Gertrude entered the throne room from the rear entrance they used, climbed the steps to the dais and seated themselves.

Laertes stood at the center of the first row of the spectators.

Ophelia, taking a deep breath, sat down in her chair.

"As you know, Laertes," Claudius said, "the sudden and untimely death of your father, our revered Lord Chamberlain Polonius, came as a great shock to me."

"Your Majesty," Laertes said, "my father was brutally murdered."

Claudius also took a deep breath. "Your father's loss is why I'm pleased to see you in court with us today. I've decided to appoint you to your deceased father's position."

The spectators buzzed. No one could recall a previous lord chamberlain who was only nineteen years old when the king appointed him.

"Laertes," Claudius asked, "do you accept the position?"

"Your Majesty," Laertes replied, "I gladly accept the position. My first and foremost task as your lord chamberlain will be the prosecution of the evil person who viciously murdered my father."

"You may take your place," Claudius said, "next to us."

Laertes ascended the steps to the throne and stood between the king and queen as his father had.

He glared at his sister Ophelia.

Ordinarily, the persons who witnessed an appointment by the king to a high position would wish to be seen and heard applauding and cheering the appointee. This time, though, the spectators in the throne room remained silent.

Ophelia's Story: Ten Years before the Visit

As soon as Laertes turned to face the crowd, Hamlet, followed by Horatio, came into the throne room. The spectators made way for the prince and his servant friend as they walked toward the first row.

Hamlet had informed Ophelia he'd enter the throne room as soon as Laertes became the lord chamberlain. His purpose, he'd told her, was to challenge her brother to immediately prosecute him for the murder of their father.

As if he were an actor taking a cue, Laertes pointed an index finger at Hamlet. "This is the violence-loving prince who murdered my father. I'll prosecute him, Your Majesty, now. I'll never enjoy anything more in my entire life than witnessing his execution before this day ends. I want to see, with my own eyes, the executioner's blade severing his neck. I want to watch his head tumble from the chopping block to the stinking, blood-caked dirt beneath it."

As the crowd murmured, Claudius glowered.

Gertrude closed her eyes and shook her head.

Hamlet reached the first row of the susurrating spectators and came to a halt. "I'm the prince," he said, "who justifiably killed an intruder in the queen's chamber. The trespasser was hiding behind a curtain. He was shamelessly eavesdropping upon a private conversation between the queen and her son. As an intruder in the queen's chamber, he was a mortal threat to the queen and a traitor as a matter of law. He deserved to die a most dreadful death. So he did, and by my hand."

"That's right!" voices in the crowd affirmed. "The intruder deserved to die!"

Laertes scowled. "My father was no intruder in the queen's chamber. He was in a civil conversation with you in the queen's chamber. He told you he'd changed his mind and would no longer consent to a filthy, odious marriage between you and my sister Ophelia. You became enraged and stabbed my father countless times with your dagger."

The queen was once again shaking her head.

Hamlet turned to Claudius. "Your Majesty, you've chosen a liar to be your new lord chamberlain. But you needn't rely upon my word alone for proof of that. I have a witness."

"Who's your witness?" Claudius asked.

Hamlet turned to his mother. "Her Majesty the queen."

Gertrude turned to Laertes. "Lord chamberlain, Prince Hamlet is right. The story you've told is untrue. Your father was an intruder in my chamber. He was hiding behind a curtain. He was eavesdropping upon a private conversation between me and my son. Prince Hamlet stabbed your father through the curtain he'd chosen to hide behind. Neither my son nor I knew the intruder was your father until the prince was done stabbing and pulled down the curtain. I wasn't happy to see your father bleed to death on my new carpet. But I would say he was taking his chances intruding in my chamber when my brave, heroic son was present to protect me."

Claudius turned to Laertes. "Lord chamberlain, you can't ask me to disbelieve the queen. I know for a fact she could never lie, and certainly not in this court. Because I believe her beyond all doubt, your charge against the prince must fail. He justifiably killed an intruder in the queen's chamber who happened to be your father."

The crowd cheered. "Long live the prince! Long live Hamlet!"

Despite the tumult in the throne room, Ophelia overheard an exchange between two spectators standing near her.

"Why do you suppose," one asked, "the old lord chamberlain was spying on the queen?"

The other laughed. "He was nosy. He liked nothing better than discovering other people's secrets—anything he could use for blackmail later on."

The king and queen rose to their feet.

"Court is adjourned," Claudius said, "for the remainder of this day."

The Visit

"Your brother," Fortinbras said, "forced Claudius into finding Hamlet innocent of murdering your father."

Ophelia nodded. "Laertes should've figured out what would happen. He should've known Gertrude would never go along with the execution of her son. He should've realized Claudius had appointed him lord chamberlain to find some other way to get rid of Hamlet. During times as hard as those in Denmark, even accomplished assassins must've been inexpensive. I mean, hiring a person like that was what a lord chamberlain was supposed to do—unless, of course, he'd rather commit the murder himself."

Fortinbras snickered. "So the very first thing your brother did as lord chamberlain was a major blunder. What kind of training for the position did your father give him?"

Ophelia laughed. "My father had all sorts of advice for both my brother and me. But Laertes reached a point where he refused to listen to him anymore. He said he didn't need any instruction from the proven failure our father was. I think that was the reason my father turned his attention to me. After all, I was to become the queen. He was certain Prince Hamlet would be an indolent, apathetic king. If I played my cards right as his wife, my father told me more than once, I could rule Denmark."

"Did you listen to your father's advice?"

"I did. For whatever it was worth, I did."

Ophelia's Story: Ten Years before the Visit

Claudius and Gertrude left the throne room, retreating from the uproar Hamlet and Laertes had created.

The prince and lord chamberlain, though, remained in their places, glaring at one another.

The spectators, unwilling to miss observing what promised to become a major escalation of the hostilities between childhood friends, also stayed put.

Laertes, grasping the handle of his dagger at his hip as if he were prepared to use it, turned to Horatio. "My friend, please do us all a great favor and remove the prince from this room. I must confess, my mind is focused right now on his death, the bloodier the better."

Hamlet, who was six inches taller than Laertes, gripped the handle of his own dagger and laughed. "That's brave talk coming from you, little lord chamberlain. I doubt there's a child more than ten years old in this land who'd be afraid to face you in a knife fight."

Hamlet unsheathed his dagger and flaunted it. The crowd gasped.

"Too bad," he said, keeping his eyes on Laertes, "you weren't the intruder in my mother's chamber. Too bad those weren't your foul-smelling guts coiled on my mother's new carpet like a nest of bloody snakes."

Laertes brandished his own dagger. "You dare to remind me you murdered my father. Come up here and fight me, asshole. I'll slice off that ugly thing you can only dream you'll thrust inside my sister."

The spectators gasped again.

Horatio threw his muscular, hard-working arms around Hamlet and turned to Laertes. "I'll comply with your request, my lord."

He walked the prince through the crowd and out of the throne room.

Ophelia sighed. The prince and brother she'd grown up with were still boys at play, still with no fear they'd become adults and bring their world down around them.

Ophelia's Story: Ten Years before the Visit

As the spectators, who'd briefly hoped for more than what they got that day, followed Horatio and Hamlet out of the throne room, Laertes approached Ophelia.

She looked at him as if he were a dog with foam at its mouth. "Despite your intense desire to want Hamlet dead," she said, "I can't help but notice he's still very much alive."

"But not for long," Laertes said. "I can guarantee you that. You'd best forget about a marriage to him. He'll never live long enough to consummate it."

"You know that would break my heart."

"I damned well know it would. All your hope in this world is to become Hamlet's wife and Denmark's queen. You'll gladly give him what he's always wanted. When we were children, he told me, in great detail, what he'd do with you after he married you. Then it was a dirty, filthy, disgusting, childish joke. Now he wants to make it real."

Ophelia laughed. "I thought a prince was supposed to bring childish fantasies to life. Cinderella's did. Why can't mine?"

Laertes shook his head. "This isn't a fairy tale. This is about a lascivious, lecherous prince who wants to lie naked in his bed with my sister. This is also about a brother who'd rather die than know the prince did that."

Ophelia frowned. "I'm sorry, my dear lord chamberlain, but I can't imagine why you care if Hamlet and I lie naked in a bed together. I understand many women and men do that in this world. And some of them, I'm told, even say they enjoy doing it."

"The thought of Hamlet's doing such a thing with you, my sister, fills me with loathing. As it should. That alone is reason enough for me to want to see him dead."

Ophelia stared at Laertes. "Even if I were perfectly willing?"

Laertes shook his head. "That has nothing to do with it. *I'll* never be willing. Hamlet will never enter a marriage with you. I'll never consent to it."

Ophelia narrowed her eyes. "Why should such a marriage require *your* consent?"

Laertes didn't hesitate. "Thanks to Hamlet, our father is dead. In his absence, any marriage you wish to enter will require your oldest brother's consent. Since you have only one brother, and I'm that brother, you'll require my consent."

"That's the law in Denmark now? An orphaned sister requires her oldest brother's consent to marry a person she loves?"

"I'm the lord chamberlain in Denmark now. I say that's the law in Denmark regarding an orphaned lord chamberlain's daughter."

"It's a special law for me? Am I supposed to feel honored?"

"You should feel honored I, the new lord chamberlain, am your protective brother."

"I should feel honored I have a brother who takes far too much interest in his sister's marriage to a prince and their consummation of it? Why should I feel anything but sorrow and pity for a brother whose mind is so filled with disease?"

Ophelia walked out of the throne room, leaving Laertes as alone in it as he was in the world.

Ophelia's Story: Ten Years before the Visit

In the throne room the next morning, Laertes revealed how he intended to restore his standing with Claudius and Gertrude after the debacle he'd wrought the previous day during his first moments on the job as the lord chamberlain.

"Traitors," he proclaimed, facing the crowd from his position between the royal couple, "have brought our beloved Denmark to its knees. Knights who've sworn their loyalty to our king have deserted His Majesty's army. Some of them have fled in boats to Norway. When they arrive in its ports, the evil Prince Fortinbras greets them himself and offers them positions in his army."

The desertions weren't news to Ophelia. Christina had told her and Horatio about them.

"His Majesty," Laertes continued, gesturing toward Claudius, "has ordered me to restore his army to its former strength and glory. I've given His Highness my solemn promise I'll accomplish that and more, much more. I've given His Majesty the king, as well as Her Majesty the queen, my pledge I'll build their army to a level no Dane has seen before. When we next invade Norway, the enemy army, seeing how colossal our army has become, will melt away like the last thin sheet of pond ice on a warm day in spring. We'll not only take back the territories Norway's ancient kings stole from us. We'll conquer that errant kingdom as a whole, from its southernmost coast to its northernmost fjords. And our army won't need years to accomplish the feat. It will do it within a matter of days."

Ophelia could hear more than a few spectators expressing their doubts about that. The new nineteen-year-old lord chamberlain's bombastic promises were, she heard one of them say, "far beyond reason."

Whether or not Laertes could hear what his sister heard, he pressed forward. "To bring His Majesty's army to the strength I envision, I'll look to the most valuable resource Denmark possesses—its people. I've therefore asked His Majesty to issue a decree today, and he, in his infinite wisdom, has done so. Pursuant to the decree, every man in this land between the ages of seventeen and twenty-five, without any exception whatsoever, will become a soldier in His Majesty's army and will begin service immediately."

Ophelia briefly wondered if she'd only imagined, as in a nightmare, the words her brother had spoken. A glance at the faces of nearby spectators, though, convinced her they were as stunned as she was.

"His Majesty and I," Laertes said, "assume all our people will wish to help their country defeat its eternal enemy. We therefore anticipate his decree will go into effect without any need for force. However, if any persons should decide they, their sons, their brothers, their husbands or their lovers can refuse to comply with His Majesty's command, then we're prepared to use all such force as may be required to field the army Denmark deserves. That force will include summary executions, without trial, for treason."

Ophelia once again found herself looking at her brother and wondering how it was possible he'd gone so wrong.

The Visit

Seeking relief from the afternoon sun, the livestock had gathered in the shade of the trees on either side of a brook that flowed through a far corner of the pasture. The geese Ophelia's family kept there honked at the calves, lambs and kids whenever they ventured too close for comfort.

"The sailors on our ships who spoke Danish," Fortinbras said, "told your deserters where to land their boats. I'd meet them there. I placed only one condition on their joining our army. They had to promise me they'd learn to speak Norwegian."

"They didn't object to doing that?" Ophelia asked.

"They didn't have much of a choice. They couldn't expect their new comrades to communicate with them in Danish. And we greeted them with food. Many of them told me it was the first good meal they'd eaten for several days. I gave them my guarantee they'd never go without food in my army. They somehow found it possible to learn a new language."

Because Ophelia's children liked to wear their mother's and father's old straw hats when they worked outside in the summer, their father told them they looked like mushrooms. When the children asked him if they'd be good to eat, he said well-behaved mushrooms were always delicious. Cooked with meat drippings, they could be the tastiest dish you ever ate. But if you took even one bite of a naughty mushroom, you'd be dead.

Chapter Fourteen

Ophelia's Story: Ten Years before the Visit

Ophelia knew the prince would pay her a visit as soon as he heard about the fiery speech Laertes had given in the throne room that morning.

The moment Hamlet sat down on Ophelia's couch, he took to grumbling. "Laertes will do anything to make himself look good. He was always like that. He was jealous I was the prince, and he was nothing but a lord chamberlain's son."

Ophelia, having been informed she was nothing but a lord chamberlain's daughter, chose to sit down in a chair facing Hamlet. "Laertes is attempting to make himself look good?" she asked. "In whose eyes?"

"In the eyes of the people, of course."

"And how will he achieve that?"

"With a victory over the Norwegians. The people would love that more than anything else. They're fed up with losing the damned war. They want what my father wanted. They want our stolen territories back. They want Denmark made whole again."

When Ophelia had greeted Hamlet at the door to her chamber, she couldn't detect the slightest odor of alcohol on his breath. She now wondered if he'd disguised it somehow.

"Wouldn't you say," she asked, "a victory like that—with all the disputed territories under the rule of Denmark's king—is highly unlikely?"

Hamlet shook his head. "It might not be as easy to pull off as Laertes says it is. But if he and Claudius are serious, and they start executing people for refusing to fight, they can put that Norwegian prince back in his place. They can succeed where my father and your father failed."

"Laertes says our knights are deserting our army. They're sneaking off in boats, he says, and joining the Norwegian army."

Hamlet shook his head again. "Your brother's lying about that. He's always been a liar. He fabricated that story about the deserters to make the situation appear to be a lot worse than it is. Then, when he turns everything around, he'll try to pass himself off as the hero who saved the day."

"I think you're wrong. I believe my brother was telling the truth about the deserters. I think our army is falling apart."

Hamlet scoffed. "What would you know about that? You sit here reading books in six or seven languages, like Horatio. How would you know what's going on in our army?"

Ophelia chose not to attempt to answer those questions.

"The Danish army," Hamlet continued, "can't be as bad off as you and Laertes say it is. If it is, then why doesn't Prince Fortinbras invade Denmark and finish us off? I'll tell you why. He knows he'd lose. He isn't stupid. He proved that when I took that phony peace offer to him. He saw through my uncle's deceitful attempts to fool him."

Ophelia was also unwilling to set forth the reasons Prince Fortinbras might have for not invading Denmark even if he was absolutely certain he'd succeed.

"The people," she said, "put a stop to giving up their sons, brothers, husbands and lovers to the army. That was after our fathers sent you to Germany and Laertes to France so you and he wouldn't have to fight in it."

"What's your point?" Hamlet snarled.

"My point is, after that, our fathers couldn't force people to fight in the army anymore. Why do you think Claudius and Laertes will succeed where our fathers failed?"

"Our fathers failed because they were too damned weak. If Claudius and Laertes use as much force as they say they will, they'll succeed. They'll win the war."

Ophelia looked at Hamlet and sighed. "It's a shame you can't see what I see."

"What's that?"

"An opportunity to win the people over to your side."

"How would I do that?"

"You could lead them in resisting the war."

"That would be treason."

"A king can't commit treason."

"What are you saying?"

"I'm saying you should seize this moment to claim you're the rightful king. When your father died, you, his only child, became the king. Claudius, the king's brother, has no right to sit on the throne. He's an impostor. So is my brother. Only a king can appoint a lord chamberlain, and you haven't appointed Laertes to that position. Their decrees and orders are therefore null and void."

Hamlet looked as if he might become ill. "Claudius and Laertes will have me arrested for treason. They'll have the excuse they're looking for to chop off my head."

Long ago, Ophelia and Horatio liked to tell their prince friend he'd surely go down in history as Hamlet the Intrepid.

"Claudius and Laertes," she said, "wouldn't get away with chopping off your head if the people rose up to save their beloved Prince Hamlet."

"Why would the people ever love me?"

"If you led them in their resistance to a horrible, stupid war, they'd adore you."

Ophelia could tell, from the look on Hamlet's face, her attempt to inspire him to pick up a pitchfork or butcher's knife and lead a rebellion would fail.

"The people might love me at that moment," he said. "But what would they do, down the road, when they decided I was no longer the king they wanted? They'd rise up again and overthrow *me*."

Ophelia paused long enough to imagine herself taking part in that uprising.

"You could easily solve the problem," she said. "You could be a good king, a king the people wanted to continue to be their king."

Hamlet once again shook his head. "You don't understand how this world is. You always took seriously what our tutor told us about bad kings and good kings. My father and mother told me her stories weren't meant to teach children but to entertain them. They were right. The truth of the matter is, the people don't want any king. They want to do whatever they feel like doing whenever they feel like doing it. They don't want anybody imposing order on them."

Ophelia could see it was pointless to argue with Hamlet about what the people wanted.

"No," he said, "I can't be making appeals to the people to save me from Claudius and Laertes."

"You intend to save yourself all by yourself?"

"I've told you before, I have to find some way to kill them before they kill me."

"Meanwhile, before you find some way to kill them, you'll kill your time drinking beer and wine?"

Hamlet ignored Ophelia's barb. "I'll have to kill them anyway if I'm going to marry you. Neither of them will ever consent to our marriage."

That, for Ophelia, was the only reason to keep them alive.

She rose to her feet. "Why don't you come back to see me when you've found some way to kill Claudius and Laertes? I'm certain I'll relish hearing how you plan to do it. Your mother's servants told me they spent a lot of time and effort cleaning up my father's blood. Maybe you and your dagger can create more clean-up labor, but this time for my brother's and your uncle's servants. They might enjoy the work as much as your mother's servants did."

Ophelia's Story: Ten Years before the Visit

Ophelia and Horatio rode from one end of the kingdom to the other. They met with the individuals who'd led the resistance to the abduction of recruits and the seizure of livestock for the army.

Ophelia said the same thing at every village they came to. "We have to do it all over again. We've got a new king and lord chamberlain who need to be taught a damned good lesson."

"If you ask me," one of the more outspoken leaders of the resistance said, "this Claudius is a bogus king. Prince Hamlet should've become the king when his father died. And why did his father die anyway? Because the person who now fancies himself to be the king, his brother, laced his wine with poison. A brother who'd do that can never be a king I need to obey."

The person Ophelia and Horatio were speaking with had used a whip to take down and render helpless, in quick succession, three of the mounted knights who'd come for her son. Her weapon, she liked to say, wasn't as lethal as a knight's sword, but it was a hell of a lot longer. It made a nice snap, too, she said, when it wrapped itself around its target.

"Is Prince Hamlet on our side this time around?" she asked.

The mother with the devastating whip wasn't the only person who asked Ophelia and Horatio that question.

"We'll see," Ophelia replied to them all.

The Visit

"You didn't want the people to know Hamlet wasn't on their side?" Fortinbras asked.

Ophelia shook her head. "I didn't think it would do anybody any good to know that."

"I imagine, though, you gave the people the impression he was on their side, but he just couldn't be as open about it as you were."

Ophelia shrugged. "I suppose the people might've thought that's what I was saying."

Ophelia's Story: Ten Years before the Visit

By the end of the first week after Claudius's approval of his new lord chamberlain's conscription decree, not one of the persons subject to the order had appeared for duty.

A servant who'd worked for Polonius and now waited upon Laertes came to Ophelia's chamber. He'd accompanied Laertes to the barracks where the Elsinore Castle knights stayed when they were on duty. The servant had never seen Laertes so angry.

Laertes ordered a squadron of twenty of the knights to pay a visit to a nearby village. "I want you to make a damned good example of all those fuckers hiding there under their mamas' skirts. They're in defiance of the king's decree. Bring them here. Kill them if you have to. Kill their mothers and fathers if you have to. Kill their sisters and brothers and their aunts and uncles, too. I don't care how much bloodshed it takes. We need to teach the Danes they must obey their king. We need to teach the Danes a certain and immediate death awaits those who don't."

Ophelia's informant had learned the abductors planned to carry out their mission as their predecessors had—during the middle of the night, when the villagers were asleep.

Ophelia's Story: Ten Years before the Visit

A short distance from the castle, the mounted swordsmen found the road to the village blocked. Dozens of individuals brandishing pitchforks and wearing bags over their heads stood in their way. Hundreds more, similarly armed and attired, stepped out of the woods on either side of the column of knights.

Ophelia had placed herself at the center of the first row of the blockaders.

"Step aside," the captain of the patrol said. "We're on the king's business."

"We won't step aside," Ophelia said. "Go back to your barracks. The war is over. Nobody else needs to die in it."

The captain grimaced in the moonlight.

Ophelia and Horatio recognized him from years ago, during the time he was in training at the Elsinore barracks to become a knight. He'd played ball games with the prince and his three friends when they dared to visit the barracks the lord chamberlain had warned them, more than once, not to go near.

"You're defying the king's decree," the captain said. "You're all committing treason."

"No legitimate king issued the decree you're attempting to enforce," Ophelia said.

"That's right!" the blockaders shouted.

"The person who issued the decree," Ophelia said, "murdered his brother."

"He murdered his brother!" the crowd agreed.

"Claudius sits on the throne unlawfully," Ophelia said. "We have no obligation to obey his phony decrees. Neither do you. Go back to your barracks."

"Go back to your barracks!" the crowd yelled.

"We're prepared to kill you all," Ophelia said. "We'll never allow you to force men into the army."

"Never!" the blockaders yelled, waving their pitchforks in the direction of the swordsmen. "Never! Never!"

The captain turned to the knights under his command and spoke to them in a low voice.

Ophelia thought what he said sounded suspiciously like treason.

"Fuck Claudius," the captain seemed to say. "Fuck Laertes. They can come here themselves and face these people."

Whatever he said, the patrol turned their horses around and rode back to the barracks.

The Visit

"You never mentioned Prince Hamlet?" Fortinbras asked.

Ophelia shook her head. "I didn't think it was necessary."

"You said Claudius wasn't the rightful king. Didn't you therefore at least imply that Hamlet was?"

"No doubt."

"Did you think your allies would've agreed Hamlet was the rightful king?"

"I imagine many of them would've agreed with that."

"And the knights—did you suppose for them it came down to a question of whether Claudius or Hamlet was the rightful king and the person whose decrees they should obey?"

"That might've been the way they looked at the situation. I wasn't discussing political and legal matters with knights in those days."

"Except for the captains you and your allies sometimes met up with in the middle of the night on their way to enforce a king's, or a phony king's, decree."

"I only met up with them because they were on their way to force young men to join the army, fight a stupid war and needlessly die. That was all my allies and I were concerned about. Whoever sat on the throne, we had to turn the abductors back—and use any means and arguments we had to do it."

Chapter Fifteen

Ophelia's Story: Ten Years before the Visit

The captain appeared in the throne room the next morning.

Laertes demanded to know why his patrol had failed to bring back a single person who was defying the king's decree obliging males of war-fighting age to join the army.

"My lord," the captain replied, "a huge crowd of people blocked the road."

"A crowd of people blocked the road?" Laertes asked. "Why didn't you make them disperse? I asked you to take twenty knights with you. Did you?"

"Twenty of the most formidable knights in the kingdom were with me."

"So why didn't you use your swords and cut through those insolent people blocking the road?"

"My lord, there were at least fifty of them for every one of us. They were armed with pitchforks and axes. Their leader told us they'd kill us all if we proceeded any farther."

"Their leader threatened to kill the king's men? Who is this leader?"

"She's a woman, my lord. She must be the same woman who led them before when they stopped us from picking up men for the army. She had that crowd whipped up. My men and I were certain they would've killed us if we'd attempted to disperse them. Some of those people would be dead and injured now, but all of us would surely be dead."

"A woman led these people? Who is this woman?"

"Nobody knows, my lord. She and all the other people wear bags over their heads. That's the way they did it before. Sometimes she wears a farmer's clothes. Sometimes she's dressed like a servant. Nobody knows who she is."

"They wear bags over their heads? They threaten the king's men with pitchforks? They're lead by a woman? That's the way they did it before? Why wasn't I told about this?"

The captain, who must've remembered playing ball in his youth with Laertes and his friends, hesitated to reply.

"Answer me," Laertes said. "Why wasn't I told about this?"

"You weren't here then, my lord," the captain replied. "I was told you were occupied with your studies in France."

Many of the spectators greeted those remarks with snickers, some even with laughter.

Queen Gertrude laughed with them, loudly. "The captain is right, lord chamberlain. You were in France. You, a true coward if I ever saw one, were afraid to fight in the war. So the king and your father sent you to safety in France at your request. Don't you remember?"

Despite the lord chamberlain's dark complexion, the crowd could see he was red with anger.

"You're dismissed," Laertes said to the captain. "I'll send out another patrol. But this one will have a brave and competent captain leading it."

Ophelia's Story: Ten Years before the Visit

Ophelia's informant again learned when and where the new squadron of knights would attempt to carry out its mission. Its destination, though, soon proved irrelevant.

Ophelia and her allies surrounded the knights as soon as they left their barracks.

Neither she nor the new captain needed to say a word.

This time, the farmers and servants wearing bags over their heads and brandishing implements they used in their work abandoned their stationary, defensive strategy. Shoulder to shoulder, they pushed forward.

Facing a screaming mob moving closer step by step, the knights knew they could only retreat to their barracks, lock the gates behind them and hope their far more numerous adversaries would leave them there unharmed.

Raising her pitchfork high above her head, Ophelia made their hope come true.

The Visit

"We could've stormed the barracks that night," Ophelia said. "We could've killed all the knights who were in them. We could've set the barracks on fire and burned them down."

"Why didn't you?" Fortinbras asked.

"The knights had families. Some of them had wives and children, even grandchildren. They had parents, sisters, brothers, aunts, uncles and cousins. They had people who loved them. Some of the people who loved them were with us. We had no quarrel with the knights. They were only attempting to carry out the horribly misguided orders Claudius and my brother had given them. At that point, nobody except Gertrude, for whatever strange reason she had, loved Claudius. Nobody at all loved Laertes."

"Not even you, his sister?"

"Not even me, his sister."

Ophelia's Story: Ten Years before the Visit

The captain of the second patrol failed to show up in court the next morning to provide the usual report of a knight given a specific assignment by the king or lord chamberlain.

Claudius chose to send his most loyal servant to the barracks. Eric showed up in the throne room for his instructions impeccably attired, as he always was.

"Tell the captain," Claudius said, "the king demands his presence in court without any further delay."

"Your Majesty," Eric said, with a bow, "I'll convey to the captain in question, in the most unmistakable terms, the urgency of his appearance in this court. I'll remind him disobedience of a king's direct order can result in his execution."

Ophelia's Story: Ten Years before the Visit

Eric returned to the throne room alone.

"Where's the captain?" Claudius asked.

"Your Majesty," Eric replied, again with a bow, "I very much regret having to repeat to you what the officer in question said to me, your most humble servant."

"Repeat it anyway," Laertes snapped.

"He told me, my lord," Eric said, "a huge mob of people, wearing bags over their heads and brandishing pitchforks and axes, refused to allow him and his patrol even to leave their barracks."

"We knew that," Laertes said. "Why isn't he present personally to explain his and his patrol's abject failure to carry out the orders the king and lord chamberlain gave him? Why isn't he here to tell us why his patrol didn't simply kill all those disloyal pitchfork-wielding people?"

Eric turned to Claudius. "Your Highness, no person should ever repeat to his king what the captain in question said to me."

"What did the captain say?" Laertes demanded.

Eric closed his eyes.

"What did the captain say?" Laertes repeated, yelling now.

Eric opened his eyes, glaring at the new lord chamberlain. "My lord, the captain told me that mob, with their pitchforks, rules this kingdom now."

The spectators audibly gasped.

Ophelia struggled, as she did years ago behind a curtain in Gertrude's chamber watching the queen spank the prince, not to laugh.

"That's ridiculous," Laertes said. "I'm certain you reminded the captain King Claudius rules this kingdom."

Eric nodded. "That's what I told him, my lord."

"What was the captain's response to that?"

"My lord, must I repeat in court," Eric asked, "what the captain told me?"

"You must," Laertes replied.

"The captain told me," Eric said, "Denmark doesn't have a legitimate king."

Nobody in the throne room dared respond, not even with a gasp, to that remark.

Eric had more to report. "The captain told me persons who murder a king can never sit on the throne themselves. They can never wear the murdered king's crown. They can never wield the murdered king's power."

Laertes turned to Claudius. "Your Majesty, I ask for the immediate arrest of this impertinent captain. I ask that he be placed on trial for treason before Your Highness this very day. I ask that Your Majesty's executioner be summoned to perform his duties as soon as Your Highness requires them."

"Lord chamberlain," Claudius said, "I grant each of your requests. We must shut this treacherous captain's mouth as soon as we can. His prompt execution will be a lesson for all the other persons in this kingdom who'd dare whisper, even in their sleep, what he brazenly told my servant."

Laertes turned to the crowd. "Every knight present, step forward now. His Majesty requires an immediate arrest."

Nobody stepped forward.

Ophelia had noticed the absence of knights in or near the throne room that morning.

"Lord chamberlain," Claudius asked, "why are there no knights present in court?"

Eric turned to Claudius. "Your Majesty, I can explain that."

"Please do," Claudius said.

"The knights told me they won't attend court," Eric said, "as long as an impostor sits on the throne."

"An impostor?" Laertes asked.

"The knights told me," Eric said, "they can only obey the orders of a legitimate king. They told me they'll remain in their barracks until a rightful king once again sits on the throne."

Laertes turned to Claudius. "Your Highness, this is outrageous."

Claudius rose to his feet. "This court is adjourned until further notice."

Ophelia's Story: Ten Years before the Visit

Ophelia followed Claudius, Gertrude and Laertes out of the throne room.

Gertrude turned to Claudius and Laertes. "I wish to speak with you in my chamber."

Ophelia hurried to her hiding place behind the curtains. Gertrude's chamber still smelled of the many pails of hot, soapy water her servants had used to remove all traces of the deceased lord chamberlain's blood.

"I never thought I'd live to see the day," Queen Gertrude said, "when the Elsinore Castle knights refused to attend court and carry out the king's orders."

Claudius and Laertes paced back and forth in her parlor. Gertrude sat in her favorite chair.

"The Elsinore knights are traitors," Laertes said. "We should order the army units at the coast to come to the castle and confront them."

Gertrude scoffed. "We'd leave ourselves open to an attack from

Norway."

"I'm not worried about that," Claudius said. "Prince Fortinbras will never invade Denmark. He's too afraid he'll lose a frightful battle. He's had plenty of time to prepare for an invasion. But he simply sits there in Norway with his army. He proves more and more, with each passing day, how scared he is and what a hollow hero the Norwegians have."

Laertes stopped pacing and turned to Claudius. "Should we call the army home to Elsinore?"

Claudius nodded. "We should. I'll send Eric to deliver the message to them."

"Then what?" Gertrude asked. "We'll have Danish knights fighting Danish knights? How do you suppose that will appear to our enemies? Wouldn't it present a wonderful opportunity for the Norwegians, Swedes and Germans? They could join together in one grand adventure to extinguish Denmark and divide its land among them."

"That won't happen," Claudius said, "not as long as I'm the king of Denmark. You worry too much, my dear. Your imagination gets the better of you."

Gertrude shook her head. "I often think I don't worry enough."

"I know what's wrong in Denmark now," Laertes said. "And I know who's behind what's wrong. I know who's behind this talk of an illegitimate king. I know who's been inciting the people—and now even the knights."

Gertrude looked at Laertes with narrowed eyes. "Please tell me, lord chamberlain, who you're speaking of."

Laertes didn't hesitate. "Prince Hamlet, Your Highness. He's the one the people, and now some of the knights, claim is the legitimate king. He's the son, not the brother, they say, of the previous king. He's the one who claims his father was murdered. Your Majesties and my father told me the previous king died because he was ill. That was good enough for me, but Hamlet has never accepted that. No, he goes around stirring up the people, and now some of the knights, for his own purposes."

Gertrude sneered. "You speak of my son. But I can assure you he's not inciting the people or the knights for or against anyone. He was always a passive child, drifting like a fallen leaf on an autumn breeze. The only times he took any action at all were when your slut sister incited him to. He's no better now than he was then. He could no more incite the people than I could fly to the moon on a broomstick."

Laertes shook his head. "Your Highness speaks of the person who murdered my father in this very room."

Gertrude laughed. "My son the prince killed an intruder in this very room. He killed a person who had no excuse whatsoever for eavesdropping on me. I'll go to my grave damned proud my son did one courageous thing in his life. The intruder could've intended to rape or murder me."

Claudius looked at Laertes and shook his head.

Laertes chose not to continue his argument with the queen.

She, on the other hand, wasn't done. "I've hoped two husbands and a son would win back the territories the Norwegian kings and princes, in the dark chapters of our history, stole from Denmark. I've hoped at least one of those husbands or that son would prove to be the hero a queen of a great land deserves to have for a husband or a son. It's been my fate, though, to have wedded two husbands and borne one son future generations will laugh at. They'll cluck their tongues and call me Queen Gertrude the Duped."

Once again, Laertes and Claudius chose to remain silent.

Gertrude turned to Claudius. "You have only yourself to blame for the people accusing you of murdering your brother. Your loyal servant, that Eric, administered a fatal dose of poison to a perfectly healthy person. I never imagined you'd prove to be such a fool. You could've paid a professional assassin to cleverly place a non-fatal dose of poison in your brother's food or drink over a period of two or three weeks. When the time came for his fatal dose, he damned well would've appeared to be as ill as we and the former lord chamberlain said he was. Even his servants would've agreed with us. You could've gotten away with murder. But no, you clumsily, stupidly killed your brother all of a sudden with one fatal dose of poison. You left no doubt in anybody's mind you were a murderer, usurper and traitor—with no right to place your hopeless ass on any throne in any land."

The Visit

Fortinbras had a puzzled expression on his face. "Here again, Claudius didn't deny he poisoned his brother?"

Ophelia shook her head. "He made no attempt to deny he murdered his brother. Do you still question whether he did it?"

Fortinbras nodded. “Yes, I do. But whether Claudius murdered his brother or not, he must’ve wanted Gertrude to think he did.”

Ophelia laughed. “And even if, in her opinion, he and his loyal servant botched it.”

Fortinbras gave Ophelia another quizzical look. “The loyal servant Eric was the person who told me, three days ago, you were still alive.”

Ophelia nodded. “I know. I’d asked him to tell you that.”

Chapter Sixteen

Ophelia's Story: Ten Years before the Visit

From the moment Eric walked into the throne room, Ophelia could tell he didn't have good news for Claudius and Laertes.

Laertes immediately began his interrogation. "Did you speak with the knights commanding our coastal garrisons?"

"I did, my lord," Eric replied.

"Did you tell them," Laertes asked, "His Majesty King Claudius has ordered them to return to Elsinore Castle to put down the rebellion in the barracks here?"

"Yes, my lord. I told them that."

"Are they on their way here?"

Eric closed his eyes.

"Speak, man," Laertes ordered. "Is our army on its way to Elsinore Castle?"

"No, my lord," Eric replied.

"No?"

Laertes had begun shouting.

"The commanders of our coastal garrisons," Eric said, "told me they agree with the Elsinore knights."

"How's that?" Laertes asked, his crimson face once again revealing his fury.

"They told me, my lord, they'll only obey orders from a legitimate king."

Laertes looked as if he'd taken a blow to his head. "His Majesty Claudius *is* the legitimate king of Denmark. Did you tell the commanders that?"

"Yes, my lord, I told them that. They told me they begged to differ."

Laertes turned to Claudius. "All the knights in this realm have become traitors."

Eric also turned to Claudius. "I believe Your Highness should know something else."

"What's the something else," Claudius asked, "you think I should know?"

"A mob followed me to the coastal garrisons," Eric replied.

"Wherever I went, the mob went."

Ophelia and Horatio had traveled with the mob.

"The garrison commanders informed me," Eric continued, "they agree with something else the local knights told me. When a land has no legitimate ruler sitting on its throne, they said, the mob rules. The knights in the coastal garrisons told me that's why they'll stay where they are."

"Treason in Denmark," Laertes growled. "Traitors are ganging up against us everywhere we look."

With a hand to his brow, Claudius stared down at the new carpet his servants had installed the previous day in the throne room.

Ophelia's Story: Ten Years before the Visit

"Denmark is going to hell," Hamlet said, even before he sat down on the couch in Ophelia's chamber. "The knights take their orders from the mob. Can you believe that? My uncle has brought the royal family to a new low."

Ophelia sat in her favorite chair, one her aunt and her friend had built from a fallen oak on their farm. They'd filled the cushions with goose down.

"This might be a good opportunity," Ophelia said, "for you to get rid of your enemies."

"Why do you say that?" Hamlet asked.

"Your uncle and my brother have no knights to protect them now."

"They still have their servants."

"How could their servants stop a determined assassin?"

"They'd never let me near Claudius or Laertes. Their servants despise me. I've always assumed that's because I'm the prince, and they don't have a drop of royal blood in their veins."

"I thought the servants at Elsinore Castle liked you. They did when you were a boy."

Hamlet sighed. "You didn't see what I saw. You *couldn't* see what I saw. The servants loved you. Horatio, too. Of course, he was one them. But they hated me. I was the prince, and they weren't."

Ophelia wondered if Hamlet had mistaken pity for hatred. After all, as he himself said, he was the prince, and they weren't.

"So you still have no plan," she asked, "to kill the usurper king and his lunatic lord chamberlain?"

"I'm still looking for a foolproof way to do it. Don't get me wrong. I know I have to do it. I'd kill myself before I'd give up on having you for my wife."

The Visit

"Christina told me," Ophelia said, "those were especially difficult times for you. She said your lords knew—all your people knew—our army was no longer taking orders from Claudius and Laertes."

Fortinbras nodded. "The lords insisted we invade Denmark. They were inciting the people to demand I make the Danes suffer for what they'd done in Norway."

Ophelia nodded. "I was holding my breath, hoping they wouldn't change your mind. Every morning when I got up, I wondered if that would be the day we'd learn the Norwegians had landed. Claudius and Laertes still tried to convince themselves you were afraid to launch an invasion."

"I have to give Christina's aunt credit for helping me at that point. She let my lords know she took a very dim view of our invading Denmark. The cessation of hostilities between Norway and Denmark had restored the volume of Swedish trade to what it had been before the war. And that's what she wanted, more than anything."

Ophelia laughed. "I never thought I'd say this, but I suppose we should be grateful, ten years later, the queen valued the Swedish trade volume as highly as she did."

Fortinbras laughed as well. "We should."

Ophelia's Story: Ten Years before the Visit

"Let the word go out," Laertes said to the spectators in the throne room. "King Claudius, in his wisdom, has decided he'll withhold all further payments for supplies to every unit of the Danish army wherever it may be. His Majesty will resume payments to a unit only after he's received absolute proof that unit is enforcing his order to seize the men in this land between the ages of seventeen and twenty-five who've refused to serve their country."

A well-known merchant in the first row of the spectators vigorously shook his head. His business relied upon supplying the army with food, wine and beer for the soldiers, and hay, oats and straw for their horses.

"Lord chamberlain," he asked, "does His Majesty intend to starve the army and its horses into submission to his orders?"

"I don't intend to starve anybody," Claudius said. "I intend not to supply an army that refuses to act like an army and obey the orders of its king."

"If people starve," Laertes said, "it will result from their acts of treason, their refusal to obey the orders of their king. Neither His Majesty nor I will bear any responsibility for the self-inflicted starvation of traitors and their horses."

Ophelia's Story: Ten Years before the Visit

Ophelia and Horatio once again rode their horses from village to village, speaking with the persons they'd worked with before in the resistance. Ophelia said she had a request for them and their neighbors that would cost them nothing.

"I'm asking you." she said, "to pay your taxes in the amounts and at the times you've always paid them. Please don't pay them, though, to the illegitimate king's tax collectors. I ask you to pay them instead directly to the army. As you know, the people and the army presently stand as one in their opposition to Claudius. And he now says he won't use our taxes to supply our allies in the army. Despite what he says, he clearly intends to starve them into submission to him. We must not let this happen. We must supply our allies in the army ourselves."

"Always ask the commanders for a receipt," Horatio liked to add. "If you have one, you'll never be accused at some future time of having failed to pay your taxes."

For a few villages close to Elsinore Castle, Ophelia's request was somewhat different. She asked the people to pay their taxes to the Elsinore servants.

"We need to keep our allies in the castle alive," she said, "as much as we do our allies in the army."

The Visit

"Christina told me," Fortinbras said, "your tax-diversion scheme was a remarkable success. The Danish army remained together. The Elsinore servants kept the castle in good order."

"Many of the people," Ophelia said, "even thought to pay the tax collectors some of their taxes. That was to make up for the portion of the taxes the collectors would've kept to support themselves and their families. The collectors had to be able to read and write and do arithmetic, but they weren't wealthy. I'd learned, though, Claudius and my brother had decided they had no obligation to help them."

"Christina told me about the tax collectors, too."

Ophelia looked at her guest and smirked. "Our people learned how to live without a monarch."

Fortinbras thought for a moment before he responded to that remark. "I'd have to say, though, your people still had a very capable person leading them—a person who could've been an intelligent, caring and successful monarch herself."

Ophelia's Story: Ten Years before the Visit

Spectators crowded the throne room. Ophelia noticed some of them were holding the doors open so the people who filled the corridor outside the entrance could at least hear the speakers. She'd never seen that done before.

Claudius had once again sent Eric to the army garrisons on the coast. He was scheduled to report back this morning.

"So, most faithful servant to the king," Laertes began his interrogation, "were you able to speak with the commanders of the garrisons?"

"Yes, my lord," Eric replied. "I spoke with all the commanders and many of the ordinary soldiers as well."

"And were you able to observe the living conditions in the garrisons, as squalid as they no doubt were?"

"Yes, my lord," Eric replied, "I was able to observe the living conditions in each of the garrisons. I wouldn't describe any of them, though, as squalid."

"How near to squalid were they?" Laertes asked.

"Not at all near, my lord."

"Not at all near?" Laertes asked, raising his voice again. "How can the living conditions in unsupplied army garrisons not be at least near to squalid?"

"My lord," Eric replied, "the commanders and the ordinary soldiers all told me they have more food to eat now than they've had in a long time. Nor do they lack for other supplies. Even their horses have plentiful amounts of hay and oats to feed upon. The stable workers in fact complained to me of overwork due to the copious deposits of manure they need to remove from the stalls every day. The workers, though, also told me they had no complaints concerning the amounts of food available for themselves. They said they sometimes wonder if the lords and ladies back home are eating and shitting as well as they are."

As Eric spoke, and Queen Gertrude rolled her eyes to the ceiling, the laughter in the throne room rose.

Laertes turned to the crowd. "Order in this court! Stop your laughing now, or I'll have every insolent laugher among you arrested!"

"Who'll arrest us, lord chamberlain?" one spectator asked. "Your knights refuse to obey your orders."

"And who can blame them?" another spectator asked. "They and their horses seem to be eating and defecating better than we do."

Laertes turned to Eric again. "How dare you stand there and try to make this court believe an unsupplied army is eating as well as lords and ladies!"

"My lord," Eric replied, "the army receives all the supplies it needs. I saw the supplies myself. The warehouses in the garrisons were filled to overflowing."

"Need I remind you," Laertes asked, "you can be punished for perjury for each and every lie you tell in this honorable court?"

"But who'll do the punishing?" a spectator asked. "The king's men ignore your orders."

"Who supplies the army?" Laertes shouted, in order to be heard above the laughter.

"My lord," Eric replied, "the people do. I saw them doing it myself."

"The people?" Laertes asked. "And what do the people get in return for their supplies?"

"A receipt, my lord."

"A receipt?"

"The people, my lord, are very particular about that."

Laertes scoffed. "A receipt for their supplies is all they get?"

"That's all they want and all they get."

"I had an older brother," a spectator chose to say, raising his voice until the crowd fell silent. "He inherited our family's vast estate. Now I realize I should've murdered him. I should've put some poison in his wine. That's all I had to do. Then *I* would've inherited the estate. And I'd be a wealthy man now. People do that in this kingdom, you know. They murder their older brothers and get away with it. Sometimes they even take their dead brother's wife, along with his property and title and everything else he might've had. And, I tell you, they get away with it. Yes, mine is a very sad story. I had an older brother I clearly should've murdered, but I didn't. What a mistake I made."

Claudius, his face as inflamed as Ophelia had ever seen it, rose to his feet and hurried toward the exit behind the throne. He never adjourned court that day. He simply fled, with Gertrude and Laertes at his heels.

Chapter Seventeen

Ophelia's Story: Ten Years before the Visit

As she left the throne room that morning, Ophelia overheard Laertes and Claudius insist upon a meeting with the queen. Gertrude agreed to speak with them in her chamber but only after she'd finished her lunch.

Laertes stood in front of the queen, who once again sat in her favorite chair. Ophelia was in her usual place behind the curtains.

"Did you hear," Laertes asked, "what that obnoxious man in the throne room said?"

Gertrude looked at the new lord chamberlain and laughed. "Which of the many obnoxious men in the throne room are you speaking of?"

"That horrid man who said he should've killed his older brother."

Gertrude laughed again. "If he'd had sense enough to hire a skillful poisoner, he probably could've gotten away with it. He was damned right. He'd be wealthy today. We'd invite him for dinner and hope he'd invite us back. We never know whose food and drink will turn out to be superior to what they serve us here in the castle."

Laertes ignored the queen's remarks. "I know who put that man up to making that outrageous statement."

Gertrude looked at Laertes as if her lunch hadn't agreed with her. "Who'd do such a thing?"

Laertes glanced at Claudius. "The king's nephew Hamlet—the same person who's behind the people paying their taxes to the army."

Gertrude scoffed. "You must be referring to some Hamlet other than the son I gave birth to, some Hamlet other than my only child."

Laertes gave the queen the look prosecutors give defendants they've caught telling an obvious lie. "Your son is the Hamlet I refer to, Your Highness. I'm sorry if this news offends you. I know Hamlet is your only child. I know you love him as any mother would love a child no matter how many crimes he commits. But the truth is, Hamlet hates his uncle. He hates me. He'll say and do anything to take us down. He's leading the people against us. He wants the stupid, lazy, wretched common people in this land to rise up against us and run us out of Elsinore Castle. The three of us will end up dead. And that's how

Hamlet wants us—dead."

Gertrude stared at Laertes as if, no longer protected by the knights usually assigned to her, she'd happened upon a madman in the streets who wouldn't leave her alone.

"So what do you advise we do?" she asked.

"We've got to reach an agreement with Hamlet," Laertes replied.

"An agreement? What kind of an agreement?"

"First, he's got to agree to give us what we want."

"What's that?"

"He's got to tell the people he believes his father died of an illness and wasn't poisoned. He's got to tell the people they must recognize his uncle Claudius as the true and legitimate king of Denmark, you as the true and legitimate queen of Denmark, and me as the true and legitimate lord chamberlain of Denmark."

Gertrude sighed. "I'd be very pleased if my son were to agree to those terms. I doubt very much, though, he'll do it. He's never wanted to admit he's been wrong about anything. He was always a willful child. Spankings on his bare ass did no good whatsoever."

Laertes shook his head. "But this time he'll admit he's been wrong. He'll do it in return for what we can agree to give him. I suspect, though, you'll find the gift as odious as I do."

"What's the gift?"

"There's one thing Hamlet wants more than anything else."

Gertrude knitted her brow.

Laertes frowned. "I don't have to tell you what that is."

Gertrude shook her head. "I'll let you put it into words anyway so there'll never be any question what we're talking about."

Laertes looked as if he too were about to regurgitate his lunch. "Hamlet wants my sister Ophelia to be his bride. He wants to penetrate her body with his *thing*. He wants to impregnate her. He wants her to bear his children."

Gertrude also couldn't conceal her disgust. "And you're willing now, in your desperation, to give the prince what he wants—your precious sister?"

"Only if that devil agrees to pledge his loyalty to Claudius as the lawful king of Denmark. Only if he tells the army and the people they must obey their lawful king."

"And you expect me, the queen of Denmark, to agree to the marriage of my son, the prince of Denmark, to a common whore?"

"Your life depends upon it as much as mine does."

Claudius saw fit to inject himself into the conversation. "My life, too. Let's face it. Hamlet has the people and the army conspiring against us. The cowardly lords and ladies remain hidden in their castles, with their doors locked. I'm surprised our servants can still scavenge food and drink to serve us. I assume they're stealing it. They know the knights will no longer arrest them, and the lord chamberlain and I can no longer order their punishment. What a dreadful time this is. We've got to give Hamlet whatever he wants. And if he wants to fuck that nasty, know-it-all bitch Ophelia, why should I care? He's got the people and the army laughing at me. And I was supposed to be the king who defeated and decapitated that damned Norwegian prince. We must buy Hamlet off. If his price is the current lord chamberlain's sister, I'm all in favor of handing her to him. They deserve one another."

Gertrude shook her head. "And I dreamed my son would marry a princess."

Laertes couldn't conceal his impatience. "But your son wants my sister."

Gertrude turned to Claudius. "I agree with you. What a dreadful time this is for all of us. I've watched two kings and two lord chamberlains take this country down into hell as far as it's ever gone. What king and queen in their right minds would want their daughter to marry my son now? All the royal families in Europe would laugh at them."

"However we got to this point," Laertes said, "we have only one course of action left. We must give Hamlet my sister."

Gertrude looked at Laertes and raised her hands above her head as if she were surrendering to highwaymen. "I'll play your silly game. Make your offer to Hamlet. I'll be eager to hear what he says. Will he agree to recognize his mother's current husband as the lawful king of Denmark—his uncle who rashly murdered his father in his haste to sit upon the throne? My son will do that? He'll do that just to share his bed with the daughter and sister of the lord chamberlains who brought this land to its current state of ruin? Go ahead with your proposed deal. The older I get the more I'm convinced men exist only for amusement. Whenever one of them appears to do something worthwhile, he must be taking his orders from a woman."

Ron Fritsch

Ophelia's Story: Ten Years before the Visit

"Laertes asked me to see you," Horatio said, taking a seat on the couch in Hamlet's chamber.

Hamlet sat down on the couch next to his guest. "You've become our faithful go-between. Are you glad you weren't born a prince or a lord chamberlain's son?"

Horatio nodded. "Damned glad."

"I thought so."

Horatio could tell Hamlet had been drinking heavily.

"So what message do you bring me from Laertes?" Hamlet asked. "His latest vow to chop off my head if I even so much as think unchaste thoughts concerning his sister?"

Horatio grimaced. "Laertes wants you to meet with him and Claudius in your mother's chamber."

Hamlet laughed. "So Laertes and Claudius can murder me in full view of my mother?"

Horatio's grimace deepened. "I asked Laertes if I can accompany you. He said I can. He and I agreed no other servants will be present in your mother's chamber."

"Good. Some of them might be glad to see the haughty asshole prince of Denmark dead at last. Do you remember? You and Ophelia were their favorites. You were always so well-behaved and polite to them."

Horatio chose not to respond to those remarks. "Laertes and I also agreed I'll collect all the keys to your mother's chamber from her servants. Then I'll lock the doors from the inside. The only people in her chamber will be you, Claudius, Laertes, your mother and I."

"Wonderful. You've taken care of everything."

"I'll serve the wine the four of you will drink to toast the coming peace and good fortune in Denmark."

"Peace and good fortune? They've been missing for a long time in Denmark. What's supposed to bring them back now?"

"Laertes and Claudius believe you and they can reach an agreement to bring them back."

"An agreement?"

"Claudius, your mother and Laertes will give you something if you give them something in return."

"That's the very definition of an agreement. Didn't our tutor tell us that? First, what will they give me?"

"They'll give you Ophelia. With the greatest reluctance, Laertes reminded me, they'll all consent to your marriage to Ophelia."

Hamlet threw his arms around Horatio's shoulders. "My dear friend, what excellent news you've brought me."

Horatio could smell the alcohol on Hamlet's breath. "The hard part of the agreement is what they want you to give them."

Hamlet released Horatio from his embrace. "No doubt it is. What do they want?"

"They want you to acknowledge Claudius as the lawful king of Denmark."

Hamlet pulled himself away from Horatio and reached for his goblet of wine. "Claudius murdered my father. How could I possibly agree he's the lawful king of Denmark?"

"Claudius, your mother and Laertes want you to tell the people Claudius is the lawful king of Denmark. They want you to tell the army and the people they must obey his and his lord chamberlain's orders."

Hamlet took a long drink of his wine. "I could never try to convince the people I support Claudius and Laertes. I'd puke up my guts as I did it. Anybody with any sense would know I was lying."

"Do you want me to tell them you reject their offer? Or do you want to do that yourself?"

Hamlet took another drink of his wine. "You'll be present. Claudius, Laertes and my mother will be present. The servants and the rest of the world will be locked out of my mother's chamber. Can you give me your word the doors will be locked?"

"I'll make absolutely certain the doors are locked, and nobody will be able to enter your mother's chamber without your approval."

"I won't need their consent to marry Ophelia if I'm the king."

"Won't you need Ophelia's consent?"

"I'll have that. I don't doubt she'll want to marry me if I'm the undisputed king of Denmark."

"How will you become the undisputed king of Denmark?"

"I'll kill the person who currently claims to be the king. I'll kill the person who murdered my father. I'll kill his lord chamberlain for good measure. Ophelia will be grateful for that. Her brother's death—no less gruesome than their father's, I hope—will be my wedding present to her."

Horatio stared at Hamlet. "Aren't you worried there'll be two of them and only one of you?"

Hamlet sneered. "Who are Claudius and Laertes compared to me physically? I haven't the slightest doubt I can kill them both with one dagger. I'd only ask you—kind, gentle, strong Horatio—to keep my mother out of the fray."

"I can do that."

Hamlet finished off his goblet of wine. "Please tell Laertes I agree to meet him and Claudius in my mother's chamber. The sooner the better. My wedding night approaches."

The Visit

"I assume," Fortinbras said, "you and Horatio were still working closely together. He told you everything Laertes and Hamlet said to him and everything he said to them."

"Every word," Ophelia replied.

"You knew Hamlet agreed to the meeting with Laertes and Claudius in his mother's chamber?"

"I knew that."

"You knew Hamlet agreed to it intending to kill Laertes and Claudius?"

"Horatio told me that. I had no reason to doubt he was telling me the truth."

A late-afternoon breeze passed through the leaves of the apple tree above Ophelia and Fortinbras. It came and went like a rumor of the tragic death of a king among a people hoping to hear it was true.

"Did you or Horatio," Fortinbras asked, "give any warning to Laertes or Claudius or Hamlet's mother?"

"No," Ophelia replied, gazing once more at her family in the hayfield.

"Did you feel you had any need to warn them?"

"I can't speak for Horatio, but I felt no need whatsoever to warn those people. It was their fight. It wasn't mine."

Turning to her guest again, Ophelia could tell he didn't believe her.

Chapter Eighteen

Ophelia's Story: Ten Years before the Visit

Horatio went to the chamber Laertes had inherited from his father.

Going no farther into the chamber than the foyer, Horatio informed Laertes that Hamlet had agreed to meet with him and Claudius.

Laertes grinned. "That's wonderful. But you've got to promise me one thing."

"What's that?"

"If violence takes place at this meeting, you must promise me you won't interfere in it, either on Hamlet's side or on my side."

Horatio didn't hesitate. "How could I choose between you? I'm your friend. I'm Hamlet's friend."

Laertes embraced Horatio. "Precisely. Do I have your promise then, you won't participate in any violence?"

Horatio smelled alcohol on the lord chamberlain's breath. "You have my solemn promise."

Laertes tightened his embrace. "You're the only person in the kingdom whose promises mean anything anymore."

The Visit

"Did Horatio tell you," Fortinbras asked, "what Laertes had said to him about violence at the meeting?"

"Of course he did," Ophelia replied.

"What conclusions did you and Horatio draw from your brother's mention of violence?"

"We assumed my brother and Claudius intended to kill Hamlet at the meeting. For them, that was the purpose of the meeting. After Hamlet was dead, they'd tell the people he'd attacked them first. Likewise, if Hamlet succeeded in killing Claudius and Laertes, he'd claim they'd attacked him first. They all three planned to plead self-defense."

"What about the witnesses, Horatio and Gertrude?"

"They'd have to side with whoever won the fight. If Hamlet killed

Claudius and Laertes, Hamlet would be the uncontested king of Denmark. If Claudius and Laertes killed Hamlet, Claudius would be the uncontested king of Denmark. Whoever ended up being the king, Horatio and Gertrude would have to say that person did what he did in self-defense. I'm certain Hamlet, Claudius and Laertes all understood that. They weren't worried either Horatio or Gertrude would testify against them."

"Did you or Horatio warn Hamlet? Did you tell him Claudius and Laertes intended to kill him at the meeting?"

"No."

"You felt no need to warn him?"

"None at all."

Ophelia's Story: Ten Years before the Visit

Hamlet and Horatio arrived first at Queen Gertrude's chamber.

Following the terms of his agreement with Laertes, Horatio checked to made certain the doors were locked from the inside, the servants' keys were all accounted for, and no intruders were in the chamber. In his report to Hamlet, though, he made no mention of Ophelia's presence in her usual hiding place.

As they waited for the persons who claimed to be the current king and lord chamberlain of Denmark, Gertrude and Hamlet stood in her parlor nervously eyeing her front door.

"So," Gertrude said, "you want to marry that harlot so much you'll agree your uncle, who murdered your father, is Denmark's lawful king. You'll force me to admit my only child—the son I once had such high hopes for—has no shame. He'll sell out his country for what he naively believes is that hopeless thing people call love."

"I intend to marry Ophelia," Hamlet said, "no matter what you think of her. But I'll never agree your present husband, who murdered my father and your former husband, is the lawful king of Denmark. Nor will I ever agree you're Denmark's lawful queen."

Gertrude shook her head. "Without the king's consent, nobody will recognize your marriage to Ophelia as lawful."

Hamlet scoffed. "Since I'm the only lawful king of Denmark, I'll obviously have the king's consent to marry Ophelia."

Gertrude considered for a moment what Hamlet had said. "Those are brave words, coming from you."

"Ophelia will be the lawful queen of Denmark. You'll be the pathetic and despised widow of a person convicted of, and executed for, the assassination of my father, your former husband."

Gertrude shook her head again. "I wish you were capable of making that come true, but I know you aren't. Except for the intruder Polonius, you've always been a lot of talk and no action."

Hamlet wasn't going to let his argument with his mother end there. "You'd best hope the lord chamberlain I appoint to replace Laertes doesn't put you on trial for aiding and abetting my father's assassination. A conviction would get your head chopped off along with your lover's. Imagine a king having to order the execution of his own mother."

Gertrude snickered. "I'm not worried about that. It should be obvious, even to you, your uncle clumsily murdered your father all by himself. The fool didn't ask me for my help."

Ophelia's Story: Ten Years before the Visit

Laertes came into Gertrude's chamber, saw Hamlet and threw his arms wide open. He strode toward the prince and embraced him. "I'm so damned glad we can be friends again."

Hamlet wrapped his arms around Laertes. "All our fighting was for nothing. It's time it came to an end."

Gertrude turned to Claudius, who'd followed Laertes into her chamber. "So you believe you and your lord chamberlain have reached an agreement with Hamlet?"

Claudius beamed at his nephew as if no issues of any importance had ever arisen between them. "Of course we have an agreement. Life will go on for us as it did before. The people and the army will obey their rightful king."

"The lord chamberlain," Laertes said, "will exercise the full powers of his office."

"And the prince," Hamlet said, "will marry the love of his life."

Horatio came into the parlor. As a proper waiter would, he carried a tray with one hand at shoulder level. Four goblets of wine rode on the tray like ships on a tranquil sea.

"We'll drink a toast," Laertes said, reaching for a goblet, "to the peace and prosperity that lie just around the corner for the Danes."

"The Danes," Claudius said, taking a goblet from Horatio's tray, "will once again know the necessity and benefit of obedience to the orders of a wise and just king."

"The Danes," Hamlet said, lifting a goblet to his lips, "will be celebrated as the people who place the highest value on true love."

"If what you say is true," Gertrude said, removing the fourth and last goblet from the tray, "the lucky Danes will have me to look up to as their queen until the day I die."

The three members of the royal family and the lord chamberlain quickly drank their wine and returned their empty goblets to Horatio's tray.

"More wine," Laertes said. "Please, loyal Horatio, fetch us more wine."

Horatio nodded. "As you wish, my lord."

As soon as Horatio left the parlor, Claudius threw an arm around Hamlet's shoulders.

"What a lovely wife you'll share your bed with," he said. "Has she let you have your way with her yet? Or does she make you wait, throbbing with anticipation, for your wedding night?"

Ophelia could see Claudius was giving his nephew an awkward, out-of-character hug to restrain him, at least for a moment or two.

Laertes, carefully observing Claudius and Hamlet, withdrew his dagger from its scabbard.

But like a shooting star in a dark night sky, the dagger caught the queen's attention.

Laertes approached Hamlet with his weapon aimed at his boyhood friend's gut.

"No!" Gertrude screamed.

Throwing herself in front of Laertes, she took his dagger to its hilt in her own belly.

She screamed again.

Loosening himself from his uncle's grip, Hamlet unsheathed his dagger and sank it deep into the imposter king's gut.

Claudius screamed.

Laertes and Hamlet withdrew their daggers from their initial victims and turned to one another.

Hamlet had longer arms than Laertes, but the new lord chamberlain was quicker than the prince. Laertes pierced Hamlet's midsection with his dagger even as he took the prince's upward-thrusting weapon below his rib cage.

"Fuck!" they screamed in unison, as if they were playing a ribald boyhood game.

Blood dripped from Laertes's nose and mouth.

Despite their injuries, Claudius and Gertrude unsheathed their own daggers.

Claudius thrust his in his nineteen-year-old nephew's upper belly.

Gertrude drew hers across the nineteen-year-old lord chamberlain's throat.

Twice injured, Hamlet summoned the power to drive his weapon between his uncle's ribs and into his heart.

Delivering a tit for a tat, Laertes stabbed the queen in her gullet.

Spurting blood from their wounds, Claudius, Gertrude, Hamlet and Laertes dropped their weapons and crumpled to the floor. Sobbing and moaning, they bled to death where they fell.

Ophelia's Story: Ten Years before the Visit

Horatio walked to the Elsinore Castle army barracks, spoke to the commanding officer and informed him he'd found Claudius, Gertrude, Hamlet and Laertes dead from wounds they'd inflicted upon one another.

He handed the officer the keys to the queen's chamber.

He proceeded from the army barracks to the Swedish ambassador's residence.

He gave Christina the same information he'd given the commanding officer.

She asked her servants to prepare her coach.

"I'll go to Norway now," she said. "I'll tell Fortinbras what you told me."

"I'd hoped you'd do that," Horatio said.

She looked at him and, despite her visitor's tragic news, managed a smile. "Did you know I asked Fortinbras to marry me?"

Horatio returned her smile. "I'm very glad to hear that. I hope he accepted your proposal."

Christina nodded. "He did. Are you aware he's no longer a prince?"

Horatio frowned. “I don’t understand.”

“His father died. He’s now the king of Norway.”

Horatio’s frown left his face like a lonely cloud chased off the sky by a summer breeze. “He’s now the king of Denmark, too.”

Christina nodded again. “If your people accept him.”

Chapter Nineteen

The Visit

Ophelia looked at her guest with another wry smile. "I left Elsinore Castle the day Hamlet and Claudius died and you became the king of Denmark. It was the last time I saw the castle. It was ten years ago today."

"I know," Fortinbras said, "ten years ago today."

"Then I learned a Swedish merchant ship brought you to Denmark."

Fortinbras nodded.

"I was told," Ophelia said, "a large contingent of the Danish army was present at the dock when you disembarked. People who were there said you were alone and unarmed. The officer sent to greet you, who was also unarmed, simply told you the army was yours."

Fortinbras smiled. "We all knew then the war was over."

"I heard you rode your horse from the seaport to Elsinore Castle. You stopped in every village and town along the way. You faced the crowds alone, without any guards."

"I didn't think I had anything to fear. I was right about that, too. In the two days it took me to make my way to the castle, I didn't spot a single pitchfork."

Laughing, Ophelia shook her head. "No, you were brave. You didn't want the people to see you as a conquering hero."

Fortinbras shrugged. "We all knew then the war was over."

The Visit

"I heard a story about you from that same time," Fortinbras said. "After your brother died."

"But before I jumped into the river?"

Fortinbras grimaced. "Before you did that. Because Laertes died without a will, a spouse or any children, you inherited your father's estate."

Ophelia nodded. "It consisted of farms. My father had collected the rent from them."

"I understand the estate consisted of twenty-five farms."

"It was all farmland. There was no manor house on the property."

"After you inherited the farms, you gave them to the tenants who lived on them. I saw the deeds myself."

"I didn't think it would be right for me to continue collecting rent from them."

"Why did you think that?"

"The tenants did all the work on those farms. My father did nothing to earn any income from them."

Fortinbras, who could've been attending events that day celebrating the tenth anniversary of his becoming the king of Denmark, gave Ophelia a bemused look. "Isn't collecting rent the only thing most landlords do?"

Ophelia shrugged. "When Hamlet's father's father was the king, he gave those farms to my father's father. They were part of a larger estate Hamlet's grandfather had confiscated from a lord who'd secretly plotted to overthrow him and claim the throne for himself. My grandfather had killed the lord and exposed him to be the traitor he was. Hamlet's grandfather gave my grandfather part of the traitor's estate as a reward for his loyalty. Hamlet's grandfather kept the traitor's manor house and the other farms for himself."

Fortinbras appeared to be no less puzzled than he was before Ophelia had begun her answers to his questions. "Many kings in a situation like that would wish to reward a loyal subject who came to their rescue. A part of the traitor's estate wouldn't be an unusual reward."

"But my grandfather hadn't been the loyal subject he made himself out to be. He was an ally of the traitor up to the moment he decided the traitor's plot would fail. Then he killed his traitor ally and gave the king the evidence he had proving the lord was a traitor. He got rid of the evidence proving he was also a traitor."

"Who told you this story? I've never heard anybody at Elsinore Castle say your grandfather conspired with the traitor."

"My father told me the story. It was his attempt to show me the world wasn't the way I wanted it to be. The people who end up at the top in the real world, he said, are the most conniving, dishonest and brutal. The people who favor honesty and kindness always end up at the bottom."

"Did you ever tell anybody else your father's story? As I said, this is the first time I've heard it."

"My father swore me to secrecy. He told me not to tell it to anybody else, not even Laertes. If I did, he'd have me killed. It wouldn't matter if I was his daughter. It wouldn't matter if Prince Hamlet wanted to marry me and unite our families."

"But after your father and brother died? Did you tell anybody your father's story then?"

"One person."

"Who was that?"

"My husband. I thought he should know why I was giving away twenty-five farms."

"You didn't tell anybody else?"

Ophelia shook her head. "No."

"Why not?"

"I didn't want anybody to contest my right to give those farms to the families who lived on them. I didn't want anybody to know my grandfather had tricked Hamlet's grandfather into giving him those farms. I wanted the tenants to live on their farms in peace, the way my family and I live on our farm here."

The Visit

"I still have some questions," Fortinbras said, "about the deaths of Prince Hamlet's father, Claudius, Gertrude, Hamlet himself and your father and brother."

Ophelia sighed. "I imagined you'd have all sorts of questions about their deaths. I'll try my best to answer as many of them as I can."

"You've given me the story the people of Denmark tell. Claudius poisoned his brother the king. Hamlet mistakenly killed your father thinking he was Claudius. Then Hamlet, Claudius, Gertrude and Laertes killed one another with their daggers in what must've been a horrific brawl."

Ophelia nodded. "I understand that's the story the people of Denmark tell."

"You added details here and there in it I hadn't heard before, but your story is basically the accepted story of what happened. Your part was mostly that of a bystander, a witness to events you had no control over."

Ophelia looked at the field where her husband and children were forking hay on what she knew would be their last wagon-load of the afternoon. She made no attempt to respond to the remarks of the king of two countries who sat on a bench with her in the shade of an apple tree.

The Visit

"As I told you before," Fortinbras said, "I've found it difficult to believe the story of the assassination of Hamlet's father. Not even Claudius could've been foolish enough to attempt to murder his brother during a social event in his chamber, with his employees serving the food and wine. A short time before that, he and Laertes had persuaded the king and the lords to elevate him to the first position in the line of succession and demote Prince Hamlet to the second position. Claudius should've known the people would assume he killed his brother. He had a motive to commit the murder. He wanted to be the king of Denmark. He also had the means to commit the murder. His loyal servant was available to give the king his fatal goblet of wine."

Now Ophelia's husband sat on top of the load of hay. He held their younger daughter on his lap. Their older daughter led the horse pulling the wagon. Despite the work their sons had done that day, they still had enough energy to race one another toward the pasture.

"On several occasions lately," Fortinbras said, "I've spoken with Eric."

"Does he deny poisoning Hamlet's father?"

"No. I never asked him about that."

"What did he tell you?"

"He told me you saved his nephew from being sent to fight the Norwegians. He was the first Elsinore servant you saved from that fate."

Ophelia turned to her guest. "I didn't save Eric's nephew. A crowd of angry servants and farmers did. I was there that night. I saw them brandishing their meat cleavers and pitchforks. They terrified the knights sent to abduct Eric's nephew."

Fortinbras shook his head. "More than one servant and farmer has told me it wasn't an angry crowd that assembled itself from out of nowhere. It was a crowd the lord chamberlain's daughter had eloquently and passionately persuaded they could do what they did."

Ophelia took a breath as deep as the one she'd taken before she jumped into the river. "I'm very glad to know Denmark now has a king who speaks with servants and farmers about things that matter. Your predecessors thought they were above that."

"I spoke privately with the servants and farmers. I haven't shared what they told me with any other person."

"I'm very glad to know that, too."

The Visit

"Eric told me his story from the beginning," Fortinbras said. "Shortly before his nephew turned seventeen, Claudius had asked the boy to join him in his bed. The boy treated the request as a joke. Claudius told him he was serious. In fact, Claudius said, he'd fallen in love with him. The boy told Claudius he had no desire to join him in his bed. Claudius told the boy he had two choices. If he became Claudius's lover, he wouldn't have to go to Norway when he turned seventeen. Claudius would keep him home in Elsinore Castle. If he refused that generous offer, Claudius would make sure he went to Norway. Claudius told him he'd die there along with all the other Danish boys who'd never learned how to use a sword. The boy persisted in his refusal."

Remembering Eric's nephew tell her that story, Ophelia turned to her own sons. They'd reached the pasture well ahead of their father and sisters and the last wagon-load of hay. And for reasons only they knew, they'd taken to pelting one another with dry cow patties.

"Claudius followed through on his threat," Fortinbras said. "He asked his brother to order Eric's nephew abducted. The king did so. If you and your angry crowd of servants and farmers hadn't intervened, the loyal servant's nephew would've gone to Norway to fight in a hopeless war. Claudius was right. My soldiers probably would've killed him."

"Stopping Eric's nephew from going to Norway was a personal matter for many of us who knew what Claudius had done."

"After that," Fortinbras said, "Eric continued to pretend he was still a loyal servant, but he actually loathed Claudius and the royal family. When the birthday party for Claudius came around, Eric realized if he gave the king a goblet of tainted wine and killed him, all of Denmark would assume Claudius had ordered him to commit what would become the most infamous fratricide in Danish history. Eric saw his chance to murder the king and frame Claudius, and he took it. And the king and Claudius, in his opinion, got precisely what they deserved."

Ophelia continued looking at her sons in the pasture. "In my opinion, too."

"I discovered," Fortinbras said, "Eric's nephew and a farmer's son you also kept out of the war in Norway are the two unmarried men you told me earlier are your neighbors here. I understand they're building a small house on their property Eric will soon live in."

Ophelia nodded. "My family and I will be glad to have Eric for a neighbor."

The Visit

"I also understand," Fortinbras said, "Eric had another reason to kill the king."

"What was that?" Ophelia asked, pretending she didn't already know.

"He wanted to help the lord chamberlain's daughter. She had reasons of her own to kill the king at the birthday party. He'd threatened to force her to marry his son. But Prince Hamlet wasn't the man she'd fallen in love with. The king's death would keep her unmarried to the prince, for a while at least. The king's successor Claudius and his ally Laertes wouldn't be so willing to assist the prince in achieving his marital goal. Besides, if Claudius appeared to be his brother's assassin, he and Hamlet would become mortal enemies. Both of them would know they'd never be safe in this world as long as the other was alive. The lord chamberlain's daughter wanted the royal family in a constant state of turmoil. She saw that as her best hope to keep herself free from a marriage to a prince she didn't love. It was also her best hope to bring an end to the war with the Norwegians she and the Danish people detested."

Ophelia noticed her sons had apparently grown tired of their cow-pie fight and now walked together behind the hay wagon like armies exhausted, at peace again. She wondered if they'd decided to behave themselves because they knew their mother was, for some reason, sitting under an apple tree in the orchard with the king—the king everybody said was the greatest warrior who'd ever lived.

"And the lord chamberlain's daughter," Fortinbras said, "had far better means to murder the king than anybody else did. Her friend Horatio knew as much about the poisonous plants and mushrooms that grow in Denmark as a professor of botany. He did a lot of his research in the library at the Swedish embassy. I'm told he read every book in it dealing with toxic herbs and fungi. And that was every book in every language he could read and write. The most important thing he would've learned was the maximum amount of a poison he could mix with a beverage that would still be undetectable to the person who drank it. I feel certain he mixed the poison in the wine that killed the old king, Hamlet's father, and framed the new king, Hamlet's uncle. And that was precisely what the lord chamberlain's daughter had hoped to achieve. She wanted the old king dead. She wanted the new king unable to govern—and in a fight to the finish with the prince she could never love."

Ophelia turned to her guest. "My earliest memories as a child include the king, Hamlet's father, sitting in his straight-back chair. He was like an uncle to me. He wasn't unkind. But he started a terrible war for no good reason. He continued the war well past the point where it became a cruel burden for the people on both sides of it. The day he approved the seizure of my aunt's steers, I wanted to see him dead. The day he told me he'd force me to marry Hamlet, I knew he had to die. Yes, I asked his brother's loyal servant and Horatio to help me assassinate him. If I'd done it merely to secure my own happiness, I might've questioned whether committing such a crime was the right thing to do. But I also did it for the people of the countries you rule today, Denmark and Norway."

Chapter Twenty

The Visit

"I have to admit," Fortinbras said, "there are a few things about the death of the king I still don't fully understand. Did Claudius believe Eric took it upon himself to kill the king?"

Ophelia shook her head. "Claudius never gave any indication he thought Eric was capable of committing a murder on his own. There were all sorts of problems. Where would he obtain the poison? How much of it should he put in the goblet of wine he served the king? You may be surprised to hear this, but Claudius thought his brother died because he was in fact ill. Eric and Horatio and I used to joke about that. Claudius was the only person in the world who believed the official story of the cause of his brother's death."

The Visit

"And yet Claudius seemed to want Gertrude to think, from the start, he was the assassin-in-chief. He wanted her to believe his loyal servant had merely carried out his orders."

Ophelia nodded. "That's what Claudius clearly wanted from the moment of his brother's death."

"Had you anticipated that?"

"No. But after the king's murder, with the benefit of hindsight, I wasn't surprised. Claudius wished to appear to be the hero Gertrude had spent her life looking for."

The Visit

"I heard the strange story about your father's death soon after it happened," Fortinbras said. "I was told Prince Hamlet had stabbed an intruder in his mother's chamber. It was the same story the Danish people told me when I came here. It was also the story you told me. Hamlet thought the intruder was Claudius. He believed it was his chance to kill his uncle. He mistakenly killed your father instead."

"That's the story the people tell."

"I suspect it's not the whole story, though."

"No, it isn't."

"You'd overheard your father and Claudius talking about eavesdropping on Hamlet and his mother. You knew the eavesdropper wouldn't be Claudius."

"I knew that. I can't imagine very many kings would volunteer for eavesdropping duty. And especially not if they had a lord chamberlain, like my father, eager to hide behind the curtains himself."

"You knew the intruder-eavesdropper would be your father."

"I knew that."

"But Hamlet didn't. He believed you when you told him Claudius would be the intruder in his mother's chamber."

"Hamlet believed me."

"You didn't want Claudius to die then. If he had, Hamlet would've become the king. He would've forced you to marry him."

"He would've forced me to share his bed and do all the things he'd told Laertes he dreamed we'd do—all the things I had absolutely no wish to do with him."

"You tricked Hamlet into killing your father."

"I never liked my father. He was mean to my mother. She was a lord's daughter my father thought was too ugly to be his wife. His father had forced him to marry her anyway. When my mother lay dying, my father would only visit her when people came to see her and he wanted to appear to them to be a proper, caring spouse."

"The servants told me you never shed a tear after your father died."

"Those servants told you the truth. My father thought he could do to me what his father had done to him. He could decide who I should marry and share a bed with."

"You also knew Hamlet's killing your father would make Hamlet and your brother mortal enemies just as much as Hamlet and Claudius were. You knew, after the deed was done, neither Hamlet nor Laertes could live in a world the other remained alive in."

"I knew that. I took no delight, though, in knowing it. Laertes was my brother. Hamlet was my childhood friend. I was sorry they'd placed themselves in the positions they were in. On the other hand, I also knew I couldn't continue to live in a world with either of them in it."

Fortinbras nodded. "I can see why you'd say that."

Ophelia looked at her family in the pasture with their load of hay and smiled. "And I wanted to live."

The Visit

"The people," Fortinbras said, "believe the story Horatio told the commander of the Elsinore knights about what happened in the queen's chamber ten years ago today. The king, queen, prince and lord chamberlain sent him to fetch more wine for them. When he returned to the parlor, he discovered they'd used their daggers to fatally wound one another. A number of servants confirmed his statements. Claudius and Laertes had threatened to kill Hamlet. The prince had threatened to kill Claudius and Laertes. None of the servants was surprised the dagger-toting queen got herself caught up in the melee. They all assumed she'd taken her son's side in it."

"I've been told," Ophelia said, "your family has never used that chamber."

"We left it the way we found it. The people come to see it and try to imagine how the slaughter happened. I'm told their speculations run the gamut. Some say, as you did, Laertes started the fight. Others believe either Claudius or Hamlet must've been the first to use his dagger. A few even imagine Gertrude kicked off the killing by attacking your brother. The people who take that point of view say she justifiably saw Laertes as a mortal threat to Hamlet."

Ophelia sighed. "I don't suppose you believe those stories any more than you did mine."

Fortinbras shook his head. "I have to confess I don't. I'm certain you and Horatio didn't want to take the slightest chance any of those four people would survive the battle they'd brought down on themselves."

Ophelia watched her husband and children approach the barn with their load of hay. "No," she said, "we didn't."

Fortinbras eyed the hay wagon himself. "Horatio turned out to be the most skillful accomplice to an assassin I've ever heard of."

"He was an extremely skillful accomplice."

"An expert accomplice. He mixed enough poison with the wine to kill all four victims with one goblet each. I can only assume none of them tasted the poison."

"I watched them empty their goblets and ask Horatio for more. They obviously couldn't taste the poison he'd put in their wine. And yet, as you say, one goblet was enough to kill each of them."

"You and Horatio also thought to bring some animal's blood to smear on their bodies after you finished stabbing them with their daggers. You knew people who die from a poisoning don't bleed much from a wound later on."

"We'd butchered a steer the previous day and collected its blood."

"Did you and Horatio have any misgivings about including Gertrude among your victims?"

"Neither of us wanted to murder her. I believe, though, if she'd survived, she would've opposed your reign as the king of Denmark to the end of her life. She hated you. You were the great warrior hero she'd wanted one of her husbands or her son to become. In any event, Horatio had to give her the same poisoned wine he gave the others. There was no way we could've left her alive after we'd poisoned Hamlet, Claudius and Laertes, stabbed their bodies and poured blood on them. She would've been a witness we never could've counted on to keep her mouth shut. And, let's face it, she never expressed any concern about the people who died in the war she championed. Or the people who suffered injuries and the loss of loved ones in it. Ultimately, we decided we had no reason not to kill her along with the others. We had to finish the job we'd set out to do when we killed Hamlet's father. And I'll be happy forever knowing we did."

The Visit

Ophelia watched her husband and children enter the hay barn with the horse and wagon.

"There's something else I haven't figured out," Fortinbras said. "Why did you want the people to believe you'd committed suicide?"

Ophelia turned to her guest. She'd assumed he'd ask her that question. "I wanted you to succeed as the king of Denmark."

She'd also anticipated she'd surprise him with her answer.

"I don't understand," he said. "Why did the people need to believe you were dead for me to succeed as their king?"

"When you arrived in Denmark ten years ago, the people knew the lord chamberlain's daughter had incited the mobs against the two previous kings. She was the woman with the bag over her head threatening the knights with her pitchfork. I didn't think you'd need a person like that around. The people might've thought they could appeal to her whenever they questioned something you did."

Fortinbras looked at Ophelia and nodded. "They might've thought that."

"I believe now," Ophelia said, "ten years later, I was right. Neither you nor the people needed me. Your rulings haven't favored the lords over the common people. They haven't favored the Norwegians over the Danes. You've even lowered everybody's taxes. Eric tells me you and your family live modestly. And you know as well as I do a country at peace with its neighbors doesn't require a large, costly army. You've turned out to be the wise king I believed you'd be."

After those remarks, the wise king sitting on a bench under an apple tree on a farm in Denmark chose to remain silent.

"I had another reason for faking my suicide," Ophelia said. "I wanted *you* to believe I was dead."

"You wanted *me* to believe you were dead? Why would you want that?"

"Some kings like to enforce the laws strictly. I didn't know if you'd be that kind of king."

"What difference would it have made to you?"

Ophelia laughed. "Quite a bit, actually. I murdered two kings, a queen, a prince and two lord chamberlains. I committed countless other acts of treason. I'm not surprised you figured out, on your own, what I did. Convictions for those crimes surely would've required my execution. As I said before, though, I wished to remain alive."

Fortinbras frowned. "But if I were the kind of king who'd put you on trial for what you did, I'd have to put myself on trial with you. I was your accomplice just as much as Horatio was."

Ophelia decided it was her turn to remain silent.

"You came to Norway," Fortinbras said. "You asked me not to invade Denmark. You told me the people of Denmark would hate me for the destruction and loss of life my army would cause them if I ordered an invasion. You reminded me I was third in the line of succession to the throne of Denmark. And if I became the king, I'd want to give the Danish people reasons to welcome me. I took your advice and heeded your request. I refused to give in to my lords who were pleading with me for an immediate invasion."

Ophelia maintained her silence.

"You and I both knew," Fortinbras said, "I could only become the king of Denmark if the three persons standing in my way—Hamlet's father, Hamlet's uncle and Hamlet himself—were somehow removed. I rightly assumed you were promising me you'd bring about their removal. And as soon as you returned to Denmark, you killed Hamlet's father—and cleverly made Hamlet's uncle take the blame for it."

"But I never had you fooled?"

Fortinbras shook his head. "Never. From that moment on, I assumed we had an agreement. I kept my part of it. I didn't invade your country. And you kept your part of it. You eliminated two kings and a prince. You made me the unquestioned king of Denmark. Together, we brought a horrific war to an end. The moment I stepped off a merchant ship onto Danish soil we accomplished everything we'd set out to do."

Ophelia looked at her guest and smiled. "That we did. But I don't think you would've had to place yourself on trial with Horatio and Eric and me. You'd be deciding your own innocence or guilt. That's why a king's above the law."

Fortinbras shook his head again. "Not this king. But I found a way not to try anybody."

"How did you do that?"

"I silently pardoned us all."

The Visit

Ophelia's husband came out of the hay barn with their youngest child in his arms. Their older daughter led the horse to its stable with her brothers riding together on its bare back.

"Besides," Fortinbras said, "the reality of the situation in this country now wouldn't allow me to prosecute you even if I wanted to. I understand all the people found out when I did you're still alive."

Ophelia laughed. "I decided I wanted them to know I'd chosen to be rather than not to be."

The wise king laughed himself. "Even if I sent all the knights in Denmark out here to arrest you, they'd never make it back to the castle alive. And I'd have my neck on the chopping block before the day was over. You wouldn't have to say a word. The people would simply rise up and save you."

"You may be right. I wouldn't put it past the people of Denmark to do something as crazy as that. But luckily for them, you're a wise king, and you'll never put them to the test."

The Visit

"I have one last question," Fortinbras said. "What story do you think our grandchildren will tell their grandchildren about what happened ten years ago? Is it the story the people tell one another now? If it is, our descendants will say the lord chamberlain's daughter heroically led the resistance to a dreadful, senseless war. But they won't even hint she murdered anybody."

Ophelia gave her guest a wistful look. "I've had ten years now to think about this. I might be wrong, but I doubt the true story, after many retellings, would remain the true story. I suspect the person who placed you on Denmark's throne would become a cold-blooded monster. Nobody could deny she killed every last person who stood in her way. And I'm afraid you'd become the monster's minion."

"So you'd prefer we never tell the people the truth about the deaths of two kings, a queen, a prince and two lord chamberlains?"

"That's what I'd prefer. You might not be the only person, though, who figures out what really happened ten years ago. Maybe we shouldn't worry about the stories our grandchildren will tell their grandchildren. Maybe we should just hope for the best, for them and for us."

The Visit

The king of Denmark and Norway turned to Ophelia's husband and children, who approached him and Ophelia but were still out of earshot.

"Will you stay," Ophelia asked the king, "and have supper with us? I have to warn you, though, my family will put you to work preparing it."

Fortinbras laughed. "Will the tasks they assign me require any skill? I was raised a prince, you know. I was never taught to cook a meal."

"I'm sure the children will be glad to show you what you need to do."

Fortinbras laughed again. "Then that's how I'll celebrate the tenth anniversary of becoming the king of Denmark. Do your children speak Norwegian?"

Ophelia nodded. "They speak every language their father and I speak."

Fortinbras smiled. "I'm glad to know the father of your children is Horatio."

Ophelia looked at Horatio and smiled herself. "The day before you arrived in Denmark, I threw myself into a river for a crowd of people to see. I swam underwater to the opposite bank. I'd picked a spot where the trees dipped their branches into the river and created a natural hiding place. Horatio was waiting for me there. I rose from the dead, soaked but unseen by anybody else. Then I did what I'd wanted to do since the day I first saw him in the royal stable."

"What was that?"

"I married him."

CPSIA information can be obtained
at www.ICGtesting.com
Printed in the USA
LVHW090557140620
657964LV00005B/923